THE DEADLY SEVEN

BY: KYOKO M

For all those who have loved and lost.
Except for the guys who screwed me over.
You suck.

The story so far…

In *The Black Parade*, Jordan Amador is sentenced to eternal damnation for accidentally killing a Seer—someone who can see, hear, and talk to ghosts, angels and demons. Unless she leads a hundred souls with unfinished business to rest within two years, her soul will stay bound for Hell. Three days before the deadline, Jordan arrives home from work one night to find a man she saw in the park waiting for her and he wants to talk. Reluctantly, she lets him in only to find that his name is Michael and he is a poltergeist—the first one she's ever met. He manages to convince her to take on his case and find out how and why he died.

During the investigation Jordan finds out from her friend, the archangel Gabriel, that Michael is in fact Commanders of God's Army in Heaven and has been missing for the past two years after being sent to Earth to find the Spear of Longinus – the spear that pierced the side of Jesus. The Spear also went missing the same night Michael disappeared, and they have reason to believe it is thanks to the archdemon Belial, who has a long standing grudge with Michael.

Belial later kidnaps Jordan and reveals that he wants to inhabit Michael's dead body because it has the power to control the emotions of all human beings. In order to do this, he needs Jordan's blood and so he plans to kill her and use her blood to open a channel into Michael's body that will allow him to access it.

Gabriel and Michael arrive seconds too late as Belial stabs Jordan in the chest. A vicious fight ensues and the angels manage to defeat him, but Jordan insists that they let her die because if they heal her, the channel to Michael's body will close and he can't enter it. The angels reluctantly agree. Michael returns to his body as Jordan dies.

Jordan awakens to find that she didn't go to Hell and that Michael is still alive. He explains that her sacrifice to allow him to return to life inspired God to wipe her debt clean so her soul is no longer bound for Hell. Michael parlayed with God to be placed at her side as a temporary bodyguard and to train her to better defend herself against demons.

This collection takes place in the two month period between Chapter 15 and Chapter 16 of *The Black Parade*. Visit the website http://www.shewhowritesmonsters.com for more information on the series.

Table of Contents

WRATH

Being Jordan Amador's angelic bodyguard against a horde of bloodthirsty demons was a lot of things, but certainly not boring.

I checked my watch for the fortieth time in the last twenty minutes. Jordan usually got off at eight o'clock. Things had been quiet for over two weeks now, which was rare for a Seer's lifestyle. She encountered ghosts with unfinished business a few times a month and that kept the both of us busy. Earlier, she had convinced me to meet her at the bus stop a couple streets over instead of in front of the Sweet Spot.

"So would you mind waiting for me at the bus stop instead of out here?" she had asked, sweeping her shoulder-length black hair up into its usual high ponytail.

I frowned. "Why? Doesn't it kind of defeat the purpose of the whole 'temporary bodyguard' thing?"

"It's been quiet for a while now, Michael. Come on. Ganking an archdemon isn't enough to prove I can take care of myself?"

I glanced between her and the store front. A couple of her waitress friends who were watching us through the window scattered as soon as I looked over. Then it clicked.

"They think I'm your boyfriend, huh?"

Jordan got really interested in her shoes all of the sudden. "Yeah. They do."

I shook my head. She was an anointed soul charged with helping the dead find peace and yet she still cared what her coworkers thought of our relationship. I couldn't decide if it was cute, frustrating, or hilarious. Possibly all three.

Then again, I could see how her coworkers would get confused when a six-foot-tall, dark-haired, green-eyed "underwear model" (which I overheard one of them dub me last week) dropped Jordan off at work on a frequent basis. I decided to be lenient for once.

"Fine. We'll give it a test run today. If you survive, I'll take it into consideration."

She shot me a scowl. "Gee, thanks, almighty Michael. I am humbled that you considered the request of a lowly human."

I grinned. "You're welcome, my humble servant."

She rolled her eyes and swatted my arm before turning to head into the restaurant. "Later, pretty boy."

"Stay out of trouble." I called, and then headed back towards the bus stop.

That had been eight hours ago. Getting off a shift late wasn't unusual for a waitress, but most times it was by only five or ten minutes. My instincts needled at me that something was off.

Sighing, I fished out my cell phone and called her, tapping my foot. "Come on, Amador, pick up."

Several rings. A click. Voicemail message. Ugh. I hung up and stuffed my hands in my pockets. It was a short walk through the heavily trafficked area on this side of Albany, New York, but it was during one of the busier times of the day. Nighttime in the city meant chatty couples walking through holding hands, teenagers hollering and chasing each other down the street, and music pouring out from the clubs already packed to the rafters with twenty-somethings.

Two stop lights, one near-death experience courtesy of a speeding cab, and one step in some gum later, and I reached the glowing red sign to the Sweet Spot. The

Southern cuisine eatery was busy. As much as Northerners made fun of the South in sitcoms and stand up shows, they sure did like the food.

I pushed the door open and smiled at Beth, the head hostess. "Hey, you."

"Michael." The short blonde grinned. "Good to see you, as always."

"Is Jordan still in the back?"

A slight frown marred her brow. "No, honey. She left about ten minutes ago."

I froze. "Left how? She was supposed to meet me at the bus stop."

"She went out back to take out the trash and I just assumed she went home after. Why? Something wrong?"

A cold lump settled in my stomach. Something wasn't adding up. Jordan wasn't the type to disappear without texting me. I didn't want to concern her friends so I kept my expression pleasant. "Nah, she probably just wandered off to window shop. I'll catch up with her. Thanks, Beth."

"No problem, sweets."

I made a point to leave the restaurant in a casual manner, but once I was out of sight, I hurried around the block to the back of the building. The Sweet Spot was part of an entertainment district in this section of Albany. There were narrow alleys between the establishments and the streets ran parallel to the store fronts.

The Sweet Spot's back alley looked like any other restaurant in Albany—lined by dumpsters and garbage cans. The concrete was littered with fallen bits of food. A couple of mangy cats fought over fish bones. The entire area stank to high heaven. I called Jordan's phone again and prayed that my instincts were wrong.

The raucous chorus to Right Said Fred's "I'm Too Sexy" echoed behind me.

I turned towards one of the dumpsters and lifted the entire thing with one hand. Her phone lay cracked and forlorn underneath it.

Shit.

I tucked her phone in my pocket, forcing myself to calm down. Think. What was my next move? Calling the cops would be ill-advised. They'd take forever, and even if they found her, there was no telling how many innocent officers could die trying to save her. I knew angels in the police department, but they couldn't drop everything for me. Better check for evidence.

Jordan had basic self-defense skills and moderate experience fighting demons, so I guessed it would have taken more than one of them to subdue her. The lack of blood implied that they didn't hurt her on the spot, so that ruled out an assassination attempt. Two weeks ago, Jordan and I had foiled a plot by the archdemon Belial and sent him back to Hell. I bargained with the heavenly Father to remain on earth at her side in case Belial wanted retaliation. Up until today, there were no attempts on her life. Stupidly, I'd let my guard down and now she was gone.

The alley was wide, but blind. It led to a small road to the right. They would've parked the car there, jumped her and knocked her out, and then carried her to it. The assailants needed to haul ass to avoid anyone seeing an unconscious woman tied up and thrown into their trunk.

I dialed Gabriel's number. It rang a few times, but he picked up eventually.

"Michael. How are you this fine evening?"

"Jordan's in trouble."

My brother's voice hardened into granite. Not surprising. He'd known Jordan longer than I had and was fiercely fond of her as well. "What happened?"

"I think someone made off with her after her shift at the restaurant. I'm there now. I need you to find the closest demon's nest to here. I'll give you the address."

"Alright, go."

After I told him, I paced back and forth as I waited, my mind whirring with theories. The average demon never kept the same nest location. They switched every couple of weeks because they knew angels tracked them. The places they used were always abandoned, foreclosed, or in rough neighborhoods thick with crime. Most demons were under orders to keep tabs on one another and dispense orders from any of the five Princes of Hell. The ones who kidnapped Jordan were probably members of the local gang of losers.

"One of our sentries says there is an old house outside the city where they take their victims. This particular establishment is akin to…"

"Akin to what, Gabe?"

He exhaled. "…a slaughterhouse. The angels with the police department have been trying to gather evidence, but all they have is missing people and no traces of the murders."

Slaughterhouse. Images of Jordan strung up and split open flickered through my mind.

"Text me the address."

"Michael—"

"Text. Me. The. Address."

"…yes, brother."

I hung up and waited, trying to distract myself with positive thoughts. Jordan wasn't some damsel in distress. She was smart, tough, stubborn, and a crack shot. If she'd been carrying when the demons came for her, I might not have been on this rescue mission.

My phone buzzed with a text message a second later that had the address. Time to go.

Under any other circumstance, I'd take a cab, but Jordan was in the company of murderers, which gave me a valid excuse to bend the rules.

I summoned my spiritual energy from deep within. Coolness billowed through my limbs and filled them with supernatural powers. Once it thrummed through my veins, I opened my eyes and concentrated on the most direct route from here. I bounced on my heels once, twice, thrice, and then released the clutch.

To the untrained eye, I'd seem like nothing more than a heavy breeze, but in reality, I was running so swiftly that not even the fastest shutter speed on a digital camera could see me. I darted between cars, around fire hydrants, on the outskirts of the crowded sidewalks between the restaurant and the demons' nest. Huge gusts of wind kicked up in my wake, scattering fallen bits of trash and scaring the hell out of several dogs. The distance from here to there was about eight miles. I made to the area in less than five minutes.

The house was at the bottom of a hill of long dead brown grass and surrounded by a high black iron fence. The exterior had been painted white at some point, but the wood on the outside was mildewed and splintered all to hell. It looked more grey than anything else, like one of those hideous places children made up ghost stories about.

The property was situated by itself for several acres, ensuring that no neighbors would ever hear the screams of their victims. I estimated Jordan had been with him for less than an hour, so it was likely they hadn't hurt her too much. If they had…God help them.

I pressed my back against the gate. Ivy leaves tickled the nape of my neck as I huddled there and sniffed the air twice. Faint scent of sulfur. Hellhounds. If they saw me, my chances of getting her back unharmed would be slim. Their barks could be heard for miles. I'd have to keep them quiet.

Gathering my legs beneath me, I leapt over the six-foot fence and landed on my knees in the cool grass. The front yard was about thirty feet from the porch. No hounds yet.

I stayed low and slunk towards the rear of the house, stepping lightly to muffle the crunch of the brown grass underfoot. I made it to the side of the house and flattened myself against the flaking paint on the walls. I peeked around the corner.

There were four hellhounds — each the size of a full grown mountain lion and covered from head to toe in shaggy black fur. Two were lying on the wooden back porch, sleeping. The other two entertained themselves with the hollow shell of an Oldsmobile. One yanked off the driver's side door and tore into the upholstery as if it were nothing more than paper. Another raked its sharp claws down the rear passenger's side. The metal screamed under its nails. It yawned, revealing rows of long glistening yellow fangs that could rip through solid steel.

They hadn't smelled me yet. I was downwind, but they'd catch my scent if I made a move toward them. Then again, maybe that was what I wanted.

I slipped my seven-inch retractable Green Beret knife out of my back pocket and cut a thin line across my left palm. Warm blood dripped from it onto the grass. Low growls reached my ears. I checked around the corner again. All of them were awake and sniffing the air, their long ears flattened against their skulls. Nothing attracted hellhounds like fresh blood.

Quickly, I scattered a wide circle of blood droplets in the grass and then stood just outside of it. All four hounds came dashing around the corner, their red eyes like deadly firelight in the dark, and they pounced straight at me.

As soon as their bodies crossed the blood lines, a flash of red light shot upward and trapped them inside the circle. They smashed against an invisible force field and collapsed into a limp, whimpering doggy pile. I extended my bloody hand and spoke the Latin incantation to exorcise them. Black smoke poured out of their thick hides and then evaporated, shrinking them down to normal size. When the hellish energy dissipated, I was left with two pit bulls, a golden Labrador, and a beagle. They sat on their haunches and wagged their tails, confused but happy to see me.

I continued around the back of the house. It was a farmhouse with three steps leading to the porch with a rickety swing and a screen door. The windows were boarded up. No matter. I wouldn't be going in that way anyhow. Demons were smart enough not to do their dirty work above ground level.

The west side of the house had exactly what I had been hoping for — an old-fashioned storm cellar door. A heavy chain was wound around the rusty handles, but that didn't make a difference. No force on earth was going to stop me from getting her back.

I pressed my hand against the rotted wood and uncurled my spiritual energy enough to sense if there was anyone home. Then I felt it. Jordan's energy signature. She was here, and she was still alive. Relief spilled over me like cool spring water.

I straightened and held my arm up to the night sky. Grey clouds slid together over the moon and darkness gathered. The wind kicked my hair into my eyes. A low grumble of thunder answered my call. Lightning flashed and then my sword flew down into my hand. Its long, narrow blade glowed like silver fire in the dark, aching to be used.

A dark part of me chuckled at the thought of what the demons would do when they found out the archangel Michael had come for their captive. The sword itself would be enough to scare them shitless — it was akin to a saber, with a thin, slightly curved blade that was lightweight and easy to wield. The handle was pure silver with patterns beaten into it depicting the moment I had cut the side of Satan and assured our victory.

Male voices reached my ears as I sliced through the chains holding the cellar doors shut.

"Hey, did you hear thunder just now?"

"No. All I hear is your gums flapping. Now hold her still. I can't do anything with her wiggling around like she is."

Don't charge in, I reminded myself as the last of the chains fell aside. *You might get her killed. Stay smart.*

The door's old hinges creaked just a bit as I lifted it enough to see into the basement. The stench of dust and rot flooded into my nostrils. The basement was dimly lit with a few naked bulbs so my eyes had to adjust. Concrete floors. Mold. Cobwebs. The room was L-shaped, with the stairs on the left and the main room towards the right. Work tables had been pushed against the far wall, along with discarded furniture. Bloody instruments crowded nearly every available surface.

There were two demons standing in front of Jordan—one chunky blond with curly hair and the other thin with black buzzcut hair. They were both in jeans and wifebeaters despite the chill of the basement air. The blond had a fresh burn scar along the left side of his neck that I knew was the result of holy water. The dark-haired demon's forearms were stained from several cuts. The skin below his left eye puffed like he'd been punched.

Jordan hung from her wrists, swinging gently as the curly haired demon came up behind her. Her eyes were half-lidded as if she'd been tired out from fighting. Dried blood crusted on her forehead, probably from where they'd knocked her out. The entire right side of her throat shone dark red with blood. Some of it had dripped onto her white dress shirt. The bottom of her knee-length black skirt was torn. Her fingernails had something brownish underneath them. She hadn't been an easy captive. Good girl.

The blond demon's hands gripped her waist. Jordan thrashed like a landed shark. Her brown eyes opened completely and she kicked the dark-haired demon right in the nose. His head snapped back, but he didn't cry out as blood splattered down the front of his face.

Buzzcut wiped the blood off his chin and spat out a mouthful. He laughed and twirled the butcher knife in his hand. Demons were built to take punishment like that a thousand times over. Jordan knew that; I assumed she'd done it just to spite them.

"Man, she's a live one," the dark-haired demon said. "She's still fighting."

"I'll dope her with something in a minute. Hurry up. That first taste wasn't enough. I'm hungry."

Jordan tried to say something through her gag. Buzzcut held the knife under her chin and growled, "You scream and I'll slit your throat."

He pulled the filthy rag down from her lips. She took a couple of breaths and then gave him a death glare. "Last chance, knuckleheads. Let me go or you're both dead."

Curly laughed. "God, I love her. The other Seers weren't nearly this much fun. We've got you all to ourselves and you're still convinced you can win."

"Not *can*, you ass-clown. Will."

"Oh yeah?" Buzzcut sneered. "What makes you so sure of that?"

"Because there's an archangel standing behind you."

Buzzcut didn't get out another word. I ran him through with one stroke. The tip burst through his chest cavity and he choked on his last breath, stricken.

Curly screamed as his friend hit the floor, his eyes so wide they looked like China plates with olive pits in the middle. He held an eight-inch bayonet knife beneath Jordan's ribs, using her as a human shield.

"Take one step closer and she's dead!" he shrieked.

"Get...your hands...*off*...my friend," I said through clenched teeth.

"Drop the sword. I swear I'll spear the little bitch like a roasted pig if you don't." To emphasize his point, he jabbed the blade into her side. She jerked in her restraints and dark red blossomed outward like a morbid rose pattern in her blouse.

My fingers tightened around the hilt. I glanced at Jordan. "Close your eyes."

"What?"

"I don't want you to see this."

She gave me a searching look and then did as I asked.

~ 16 ~

"Last warning. Back away from her."

"And I told you to—AAAAGH!"

I sliced his right arm off at the shoulder. The bayonet and his arm hit the floor with a sickening thud. Blood sprayed all three of us. Curly, still screaming, stumbled away from Jordan. I took a stance in front of her.

"You son of a bitch!" the demon spat as he fumbled for the knife still clasped in his dismembered hand. "I'll kill you!"

He ran at me with the weapon aloft, aiming for my head. I caught his wrist on the downward stroke and shoved the sword through the space above his collarbone. He jerked forward and twitched, staring at me from inches away. Fear filled those beady eyes, followed by panic. Blood oozed from the wound, joining the widening puddle made by his severed arm.

A nasty chuckle escaped my lips. "Congratulations, demon. You have finally managed to piss me off."

I tightened my grip on his wrist and broke it. He cried out again. I savored the sound. I kicked his left kneecap and he collapsed in front of me. I left the sword where it pierced him instead of going for the killing blow. He broke into violent shudders. More blood welled from between his lips and spilled down his front.

"You must have heard by now what happened with Belial. He set his sights on this woman and thought he could just take what he wanted from her. He was sorely mistaken, as you are right now."

I grabbed a handful of his hair and jerked his head back so he'd have to look up at me. "She restored my life. Without her, I'd be walking the earth lost and alone. You must understand how it makes me feel that you've got her strung up like some bovine carcass."

"D-Didn't know…you were…protecting her…" the demon stammered in between wet gulping breaths. "Just thought she was…alone…"

"But that's what you do, isn't it?" I said, casually twisting the blade a bit just to watch him cringe. "You stalk and you feast on those that you think are your prey without considering the consequences."

I ripped my sword out of his chest and then kicked him in the sternum. He fell onto his back. I jammed the tip of the blade through his left hand, pinning it to the floor. He bucked upward with convulsions and a whimper crawled out of his throat.

"P-Please just k-kill me. I'll never t-touch another Seer again. I s-swear!"

"Why should I show you mercy? You weren't going to do the same. Maybe I should just cut loose. No one will find you here. I could lay into you for hours. Make you a tourniquet for that arm and slice you open. See what makes you tick. Pull your soul out of that fat dump of a body and toy with it until I've had my fill. Does that sound fun to you, demon?"

I shoved the sword an inch deeper into the punctured mess in his hand and he yowled like a beast with its leg in a bear trap.

Then Jordan spoke from behind me.

"Michael, please."

Just those two words were like a bucket of ice water dumped over my head. I realized what I'd been doing. Her safety was far more important than my desire for revenge. Still, I couldn't let this slimy bastard think I'd gone soft.

"Take this message to your people, you obsequious little worm," I murmured. "Anyone who lays a hand on

Jordan Amador will have to answer to me. Now do me a favor and *go to hell*."

I removed my sword from his hand and then decapitated him in one swift movement. His severed head tumbled across the floor like a wayward bowling ball. Good riddance.

I set my sword aside, found a stool in the corner, and climbed up in front of Jordan. Her handcuffs were attached to a huge meat hook bolted into the ceiling. I lifted her off of it with great care, unsure if she had the strength to stand. As soon as her arms were free, she looped them around my shoulders and pressed her face against my neck. She was trembling, but not crying. I sank to the floor and cradled her in my lap, breathing out the last of my anger now that she was safe.

"'M sorry," she mumbled in a small voice. "I'm so sorry, Michael."

I snorted. "What the hell do you have to apologize for? You got kidnapped. Pretty sure that's not your fault."

She shook her head, her words partially muffled as she pressed her face against my shirt. "Should've been stronger. I could've gotten you killed."

"By Heckle and Jeckle here? Not likely."

A shaky laugh rattled through her. She slid her fingers into the hairs along the nape of my neck and hugged me tighter. I knew from experience she didn't want me to see her face because she knew she was only seconds away from breaking down. No one would ever accuse Jordan Amador of being a crybaby, not if she could help it. It was a ridiculous notion at best, but I indulged her anyway.

"Thank you."

"Just doing my job. But you're welcome."

I smoothed the sweaty hairs away from her forehead enough to kiss it. She didn't move away. We stayed there for a while without speaking, just clinging to each other until we felt strong enough to separate.

Thankfully, aside from some bruises and the wound on her neck, she wasn't badly hurt. I broke her out of the cuffs and healed her before setting about to clean up our mess.

The demons had a huge compost heap in the backyard for disposing the unsavory bits of their victims, complete with copious amounts of lye. I dumped the bodies and then spread a liberal amount of lye on the corpses. Jordan didn't say anything, but she had no trouble helping me haul the bodies. She had seen her share of the dead, enough to last her a lifetime, I was sure.

I ended up gathering our bloodstained shirts together in a metal garbage pail and burning them. Nothing I knew of could get that much blood out. We didn't know if more demons would show up so there wasn't enough time to clean up in the bathroom upstairs. I found Jordan's duster balled up in the corner of the basement. Thankfully, it hid the residual stains on her upper body.

We caught a cab back to her apartment. She didn't eat anything for dinner, and I wasn't surprised. Instead, she slipped into the bathroom and took a long shower. I called Gabriel to let him know the matter had been resolved. He promised to drop by and see her in the morning.

Her bedroom door opened. I glanced over. She stood there with damp unkempt hair and oversized white Daffy Duck t-shirt. I couldn't identify the warm feeling blossoming inside my chest. It was probably for the best.

"Feeling any better?" I asked as I stood up from the couch.

She shrugged. "As good as I'm going to feel right now."

I nodded towards the rumpled covers on her bed. "Get some rest."

I turned to walk away, but then she caught the hem of my shirt. I turned again. She immediately let go and stared at her bare feet.

"I know it's a lot to ask, but would you…"

I smiled. "Yeah."

She walked back into the bedroom. I shut the door and kicked off my shoes and socks. Jordan crawled onto the mattress and curled up on the left side. I settled down on the right. She pulled the covers up over her shoulders. I lay on my back, staring at the ceiling fan blades whirling above us.

I couldn't tell how long I'd been lying there, but sometime later the mattress moved next to me. I cracked open an eyelid to check on Jordan. She was curled up in the fetal position and shivering despite still being under the covers. *Shit.*

I scooted closer and touched her shoulder. She flinched, but didn't wake up. She was a heavy sleeper, after all.

I stroked the length of her arm for a moment or two. Gradually, the shaking slowed. After a minute, it stopped altogether. Her lithe body uncurled a little and the tension in her limbs vanished. There was still a lot I didn't know about this girl.

Once I was sure she was okay, I grabbed an extra pillow from the closet. I got back in bed, wedged it between our lower bodies, and then wrapped an arm around her waist. As soon as she felt my presence, she snuggled her back against my chest without ever waking. I had figured as much. She'd been in a long term relationship before she met me, and some habits never wore off. It wasn't until the next morning that I realized something startling.

I had never slept better.

WRATH II

A lifetime of fighting monsters taught me one thing most of all—sometimes the ghosts that followed us around were our own, ones we created from the fragments of our worst sins and our worst memories.

Jordan and I got off work around the same time, so we grabbed dinner at an Italian place her best friend Lauren had recommended. We were both a bit tired at first, but the succulent scent of seared seafood, pan-fried beef, homemade marinara, melted cheese, and freshly baked garlic bread eradicated our exhaustion.

"I swear," Jordan said through a mouthful of linguine. "If you steal another piece of shrimp off my plate, I will shank you with my fork."

I popped the pilfered crustacean into my mouth. "I forget how violent you get over food sometimes."

She stole a piece of my veal Parmesan in retaliation. "Sleep with one eye open."

"I always do."

I noticed that she winced as she settled back in her chair. My gaze immediately dropped to her chest to the wound hiding beneath her white button-up shirt. It was still new enough to sting when she bent in certain positions. The stitches wouldn't come out for a while, and I knew they had to hurt.

"You okay?" I asked in a slightly softer tone.

She waved a hand to dismiss the comment. "Fine. I promise."

Part of me wanted to probe further into the way she brushed off my concern, but I knew she had at least been sleeping better. Jordan's dark complexion always told the truth. She got bags under her eyes when she didn't sleep, and her brown skin looked dry when she was stressed. Right now, her face practically glowed in the mood lighting. It had been over a week since her kidnapping, but she bounced back with an admirable resilience.

Jordan nodded towards me. "What about you? How are you adjusting to the ho-hum life of a struggling musician?"

I sipped my Cabernet, then shrugged. "I'm used to it, at least."

Her face shifted into a thoughtful expression. "Do you miss it?"

"What?"

"Heaven."

I set the wine glass on the table. "That's kind of a rhetorical question, isn't it?"

"True," she admitted. "I mean, it is paradise. Do you visit when I'm not around?"

"There hasn't been a need, no. It's not like anything ever changes up there, except for new tenants."

She sighed, leaning her head on her hands. "I wish you could tell me what it's like. All I have to go on is fiction, and whatever bits and pieces we cobbled together in the Bible. You're so fortunate. You've seen all kinds of things I'll never know about."

I smiled. "Well, look at it this way. Your soul is free again. At least now you have the opportunity to see what it's like."

Jordan swirled the straw in her pink lemonade, her voice surprisingly shy. "What do you think my chances are of getting in?"

I let her sweat it out for a good fifteen seconds and then answered. "You're ridiculously surly, but I think you've got a good shot."

I leaned forward and winked. "But if you're nice to me, I'll put in a good word for you with the Old Man."

She laughed. "I'll keep that in mind."

I started to take another sip of my wine, but then I felt it—a cold spot blooming through my chest like internal frostbite. My eyes darted through the restaurant to detect what had set off the alarms on a supernatural level.

We were seated in the middle of the dining room about ten feet from the entrance to the restaurant. There were people outside chatting and smoking, but one young light-skinned black girl stood stock still in front of the window, staring at me. I knew the second our eyes met what she was. A lost soul. A ghost.

I exhaled. So much for the rest of my night. "Better finish up. We've just caught a case."

Jordan frowned. I guided her gaze to the window. Once she spotted the dead girl, she wolfed down the remainder of her entrée and I signaled our waitress for the check. A few minutes later, we left the restaurant and motioned to the girl so she'd follow us.

The three of us walked to the rear of the parking lot where there weren't any people, just spotty overhead lights and empty cars. After the hellish business with Jacob, an evil child poltergeist, I stayed cautious around the undead and I'd instructed Jordan to be the same way. We both stood a healthy few feet apart from the girl, just to be safe.

She was about five-foot-four with short hair, her bangs dyed fire-truck red while the rest was jet-black. A few freckles dotted her nose. Her frame was scrawny, as if she'd been either anorexic or underfed, not simply slender. She wore a yellow rain slicker, a black t-shirt with the Deadpool logo on it, and blue jeans. Like all ghosts, she had no feet as her soul was suspended between Earth and the worlds beyond, no longer bound by the standard rules of life and death.

Jordan spoke first. "My name is Jordan. I'm a Seer, which means it's my job to help spirits find peace. Do you remember your name?"

"It's Lydia," the girl said in a meek voice, wringing her hands. "I...can't remember my last name."

"That's alright," I said as soothingly as I could. "I'm Michael. I'm an archangel. I can also help you find your way."

She blinked her large brown eyes rapidly. "A-An archangel? Wow. So all that heaven and hell stuff people are spouting is the real deal?"

"I know, right?" Jordan said with a grin as she fished her pen and miniature writing pad from the pocket of her oversized grey duster. "Who knew? But back to you. Can you recall where you're from or how you found us?"

She pointed to the west. "I came from this direction. Not sure how far, though. I think the first thing I passed was some fancy shoe store. I don't know, I just...felt compelled to find you for some reason."

"It's an inherent thing," I told her. "Do you know why you stayed behind? Any family or friends you want to say goodbye to?"

"I'm not sure."

"What's your last memory? Take your time and concentrate."

Lydia closed her eyes, wrinkling her brow. "It was cold and raining. I got mud all over my shoes. Something in my hands, maybe a shovel."

"That's good," Jordan said, scribbling. "The last time it rained was the day before yesterday. Was anyone with you at the time?"

The ghost girl shook her head. "Not that I know of."

"We'll start with the obituaries and missing person reports," I said. "Hopefully, something will turn up. Don't worry. We'll get this worked out, okay?"

Lydia offered me a nervous smile. "Thank you."

We headed back to the main boulevard and let Lydia walk ahead to see if any of the places nearby jogged her memory. The pedestrians passed right through her as if she weren't there and didn't feel the icy sensation that Seers and angels did whenever they touched a human soul. Normal people were lucky that way.

"I don't get it," Jordan murmured to me. "She can't be a day over fourteen. What could have possibly made someone like her drop dead?"

"We don't know her background yet," I replied. "Could be something terminal. Could be suicide. Could be an accident."

Jordan shook her head, and her high ponytail wagged back and forth. "Can't you feel it, though? That rotten gut feeling?"

I stared at her solemn frown and then glanced at Lydia. She had a point. I didn't get a sense of anything sinister from Lydia, but the shovel and rain story didn't sit well with the veal and wine in my belly. Jordan's instincts usually proved right. A storm rumbled on the horizon, too far to make out just yet, but we could almost smell the incoming rain.

Lydia stopped in front of said expensive shoe store. "I think I was here when I woke up."

"Well, I doubt your body is in there," Jordan said. "We'd better ask if anyone recognizes you."

I held the door for the ladies and we walked in. A blond guy in his mid-twenties greeted us. The shop was relatively small, with about twelve shelves split in half on either side and shoes lining the far walls. It was near closing time so the shop was empty aside from an older lady and her daughter.

"I know this might be an odd question, but we're looking for a friend of ours," I told him. "Name's Lydia. Short, red-and-black hair, freckles, light-skinned? She might have been through two or three days ago."

He paused. "Actually, she sounds familiar. She bought a pair of brown leather boots with us. Paid cash for them, which is rare since they were three-hundred-and-fifty dollars. Most people use credit cards for such large purchases."

Damn. Cash meant he wouldn't have captured any of her information, like a billing address or learner's permit. "Was she a repeat customer?"

"I believe so. Let me check with one of my coworkers, if you'll excuse me for a moment."

He walked over to the plump dark-haired woman helping the mother and daughter. Lydia's posture became anxious as she spotted the woman.

"I think I know that lady. I feel like maybe she was someone I talked to right before…" Lydia bit her bottom lip, as if she were hesitant to say "I died" out loud. Poor thing.

I watched the woman's demeanor as the sales clerk explained the situation. Worry wrinkled her brow, and not in the suspicious kind of way. She seemed concerned, not skittish.

She came over after politely excusing herself from her customers. "I'm Karen. What seems to be the problem? Has Lydia gone missing?"

Jordan and I exchanged glances. "What makes you say that?"

"I know her. Lydia's a sweetheart. She's been saving up for a pair of boots she really wanted over the past month. I got the impression from our interactions that she comes from a broken home. She doesn't get allowance from her father. The money she saved was from little odd jobs she picked up here and there: yard work, housecleaning, those sorts of things."

"Did you ever get her last name?" Jordan asked.

"Yes. I talked her into a rewards card to help knock ten percent off her purchase. I'll pull it up."

We followed her over to the left where the register was. Jordan wrote down Lydia's full name and address. Lydia said nothing the whole time, but the fond look she gave the older woman confirmed what she'd said.

"Can you..." Karen licked her lips, as if considering what to say. "Can you keep me in the loop? She's not much older than my daughter. A kid like that needs someone looking out for her."

Guilt welled up in my chest. It hurt that much more considering the ghost of the girl stood right next to her and she couldn't see her. I touched her shoulder. "Yeah. We'll let you know what we find. Thanks for your help."

"You're welcome."

The three of us left the store. Lydia piped up not long after we hit the sidewalk in search of a cab. "I don't understand. If I didn't die here, why is this the last place I remember?"

"Your memories are fluid because of the state of your soul," I said. "You might not remember it all in chronological order—just things that were important to you. Karen said you might have come from a broken home. It seems she made you happy, so you were naturally drawn to her."

A cab pulled up alongside us and we climbed in. Jordan gave him the address—a house on the outskirts of downtown Albany in the suburbs—and then we were off. I remained quiet during the ride, considering what we had learned so far. The case now relied on Lydia's father—who he was, what he did, and his attitude once we talked to him, if he'd even allow it. If her death was unnatural, it was likely he was involved, but I had to stay objective just in case.

However, I set about searching through the local obituaries on my phone while the girls talked.

"Do you remember anything about your father yet?" Jordan asked Lydia.

The girl shook her head. "No. Maybe it'll help when I see him."

Fifteen minutes later, we pulled up to a two-story house at the end of a cul-de-sac. No lights on. A rusted mauve Lincoln sat in the driveway. A waist-high picket fence hemmed in a yard of overgrown grass. Half-dead shrubs added to the overall daunting appearance.

After sending the cab away, I reached over the fence and felt about for the latch, unlocking it to let us in. As soon as it swung inward, a loud bark echoed near the tree to our left. A big brown pit bull leapt to its feet and ran straight at me. I tensed for a fight, but Lydia darted in front of me, crying out, "Boomer, no!" as if on instinct.

The dog immediately halted in front of the ghost and sniffed her outstretched hand. Few people knew that dogs, cats, and even some horses were sensitive to the supernatural. After a moment, Boomer sat on his haunches and wagged his tail, happy to see his owner even though she was no longer alive.

"Who's out there?" a growling male voice called out from the screen door. I looked up to see a black man in his early fifties scowling at us. He wore a beer-stained wifebeater beneath a black-and-blue flannel shirt and jeans. Grey clustered around his temples and throughout his goatee.

Jordan stepped forward. "Sorry, we didn't mean to intrude. We wanted to ask about your daughter, Lydia."

He stared us down for a handful of seconds, stone-faced. "You found her?"

"Found her? You knew she was missing?"

"She ran off again. Last night sometime. I already called the police."

Jordan glanced at me. I gave her a small shake of my head. Lydia wasn't mentioned in any of the missing persons ads. He was lying.

"We think we might have found something," I said, taking the lead. "Can we come in to discuss it?"

The old man eyed us and then noticed how the dog wasn't barking. "Alright, fine, but be quick about it. I'm heading out to look for her in just a few minutes."

Jordan pulled the door open and waited until I was right behind her before murmuring to me. "I'll keep him talking. Get Lydia walking around to see if she remembers anything."

I nodded and beckoned the ghost after she came in after me. Jordan and the father went through the archway to my left into the den. I shut the door and kept my voice low as I addressed Lydia. "Take a look around and tell me what you remember. Anything at all, no matter how trivial."

The foyer was small and led to the kitchen straight ahead. I overheard Jordan introducing herself and found out the father's name was Lester. She continued engaging him with the story about the boots Lydia had bought.

Lydia took small, unsteady steps through the foyer to the kitchen, her brown eyes glittering with tears. She stopped in front of the sliding glass door that exposed the backyard. A few trees lined the rickety fence and an old, worn swing set sat to our right.

"I...remember now. My mom, she...died a year ago. Car crash. She was the only thing holding this family together. After she was gone, my dad just lost it. Starting drinking and using again like he did when he was in his twenties. I tried to take care of him, but he wouldn't let me because he said I reminded him too much of my mother. He hasn't been able to keep a job, so the bank was closing in on our house."

She wrapped her arms around her stomach, trembling. "Then, the night before last, I heard about someone knocking over a gas station a couple miles from here. When I got home from school, there was a little tree in the backyard I'd never seen before."

Lydia pointed to the crabapple tree to the left with freshly turned dirt surrounding it. "He wasn't here so I got a shovel and I dug it up. I found a huge bag of bills, a gun, and a ski mask."

She faced me, tears streaming down her face. "I didn't know what to do. I mean, he was my father. He needed the money, but...one of those store clerks got shot trying to get the gun away from him. He was a nice man. He didn't deserve to die."

I stepped close to her. "Lydia, what happened after that? Tell me."

Her upper body quaked with sobs as she struggled to speak. "It was cold and wet. I heard something behind me. When I turned around, he was there and he had a baseball bat. That's the last thing I remember."

I closed my eyes. *Son of a bitch.*

"Stay here."

I walked into the den with my hand in my back pocket, resting on the knife just in case things broke bad. The couch was shrink-wrapped. Assorted boxes covered the floor. The walls were bare. He was going to skip town, the coward.

Jordan and Lydia's father were still talking, but they turned to look at me when I entered the room.

"We should get going," I said, trying my best not to sound concerned. "Hopefully, something will turn up. Good luck to you, sir."

He nodded and grunted. As soon as we were out the door, I whirled on Jordan. "Lydia remembered her death. It was him."

Rage flooded the Seer's features. "That bastard. He's already got everything packed up and he's gonna go on the run if we don't stop him."

"I know." I handed her my knife. "Slash his tires. That will at least slow him down. I'll call for backup."

I had only taken one step beyond the threshold when the cold metal of a gun pressed to the back of my neck. "That's not gonna happen, white boy."

I froze. Jordan stayed where she was on the porch, her eyes wide as she spotted Lydia's father behind me.

"Both of you step back inside this house. You call out for help or try to run and I blow his brains out."

Jordan's gaze lowered to the knife in her hand and then up to me. I gave her the tiniest shake of my head that I could manage and began to back into the foyer. She followed slowly, her eyes trained on the killer.

"Shut the door," Lester ordered.

Jordan obeyed. "Now drop the knife and kick it over to me."

She clenched her jaw, but did as he ordered.

He pocketed the knife, then started patting me down, keeping the barrel aimed at my skull the entire time.

"I knew it," he said after he was finished. "You aren't cops. So who the hell are you? Social workers? Reporters?"

"It doesn't matter," I said. "This isn't going to work. You need to turn yourself in before things gets out of hand."

"We're too late for that!" he spat. "A year too damn late. I didn't want to kill Lydia, but she left me no choice."

"No choice," Jordan breathed, her hands balling into fists. "She was your *daughter*. You had plenty of choices, but you chose to take her life just to cover up your own selfish crime."

"You don't know what I been through! I lost my wife. I lost my job. I lost everything. Then I had to come home to her, looking up at me with those eyes..." A harsh sound escaped him that was similar to a sob. "Those eyes just like Connie's. Telling me over and over that I failed her. I couldn't take it anymore. I had to do it so I could start fresh. Somewhere new. Somewhere I could forget the past."

The gun barrel trembled against my nape. He was losing composure. All it took was one tiny pull and I'd be down for the count—unconscious, not dead with a regular gun—so I needed an opening to disarm him. Still, Jordan was right in the line of fire if I went for the gun. I'd have to shield her from it.

"You can't forget the past!" Jordan shouted, alarming me right out of my thoughts. "You can't erase it or change it or dress it up. You did this to Lydia and you will never be able to escape it no matter how far you run."

"Shut up!" The older man hollered back. "I got a new start waiting for me and I'm not going to let you two stop me."

Jordan let out a malevolent laugh. "Then you better shoot me, because if you don't, I swear I will put you in the ground."

"Jordan," I said quietly. "Calm down. Let me handle this."

Her shoulders heaved with every breath and I caught a glimpse of something dark and fierce in her eyes. Then it dawned on me. She probably couldn't even see him anymore. The abusive relative, the poor living conditions, and the young girl were pieces of a puzzle, and that puzzle was Jordan's past. She was reliving it right in front of me.

I addressed Lester instead. "Listen to me. There's still a chance to end this without any more bloodshed. Give me the gun."

"No. I'm not going to jail. You shouldn't have come here. Now I have to get my hands dirty one last time before I—"

I whirled, grabbing the gun barrel and twisting it to the side, away from both me and Jordan. It went off three times, punching holes in the front door. I hit Lester in the temple with a brutal punch, but the old man had anticipated the move. He stabbed me in the gut with my own knife. Sharp, agonizing pain ate through my belly and crawled up my chest.

I stumbled backwards and hit the floor, struggling to breathe. The gun tumbled out of my slackened grip and hit the ground between us. Lester dove for it, but Jordan got there first.

"How does it feel?" she murmured, standing over him. "Tell me how it feels looking up at the barrel of a gun, knowing it's just seconds from wiping you off the face of the earth, you sorry bastard."

"Jordan," I croaked. "Don't."

"He deserves it. He deserves it a thousand times over."

I gritted my teeth and pulled the knife out of my side. Blood painted the blade scarlet all the way to the hilt. If I were human, it would have been a fatal wound. But I wasn't.

"I know he does," I said, using the handrail from the stairwell to pull myself up. "But that's not why we're here. We're not here for revenge. We're here for justice. We're here to help a little girl."

"How is this fair?" she whispered. "She'll never get to live out her dreams and yet this piece of shit is still alive."

I took a couple unsteady steps towards her, hardening my voice. "It's not about fairness, Jordan. It's about doing the right thing. I know what you're feeling right now. Rage. It's like a drug. If you let it, it'll destroy you. I can't let you go down that path. I won't."

At last, I came up to her right side, one hand staunching the blood oozing from the stab wound, the other outstretched. "Give me the gun."

She kept staring at the pathetic murderer on the floor, her arms steady, her finger on the trigger, saying nothing.

"Look at me, Jor."

She met my eyes. "He's not worth it. You don't need to do this for her or for yourself. Now give me the gun."

Silence pervaded the room. Then, slowly, she eased her finger off the trigger and handed the weapon over. She brushed past me, heading towards the backyard, wiping her face along the way. Once she left the room, I took out my cell phone and called the angels in the homicide department.

Thirty minutes later, Lester was in police custody and Lydia's body was recovered from the pit he'd dug for her in the backyard. Lydia's final wish was to figure out how she died, and who did it, so I was able to help her cross over not long after we exhumed her body.

After I wrapped everything up with the cops and got myself healed, I returned to the ruined backyard to find my partner. Jordan sat on the swing set, her hands on the rusted chains, toes skimming the grass, staring at the hole where Lydia died. She wasn't crying, but her eyes were red.

I sat down on the swing and clasped my hands, not knowing what to say just yet. Crickets chirped around us. Something rustled in the trees along the side of the fence. Under any other circumstances, the natural sounds of nighttime in the suburbs would be comforting.

"I'm sorry," she said. "I didn't mean to lose it back there."

"Couldn't be helped. This one hit close to home for both of us."

She shook her head. "I wanted to kill that man, and I still want to for what he did. She was just a kid."

"I know. Believe me, I know. I wanted to let you do it."

She looked at me then. The sorrow and regret in her delicate features made her appear years younger. "But you didn't. You stayed strong. You did the right thing. How do you do that in the face of such ugly situations like this?"

I stared out into the darkness of the yard as the wind blew through it, sending dead brown leaves dancing in circles. "I can see the big picture. For all the suffering in the world, there are also so many beautiful things that make up for it."

She snorted. "Yeah, like what?"

"The Caribbean ocean at sunrise. A baby taking its first steps. A complete stranger saving someone's life. You dancing around in your kitchen while singing the *Sweeney Todd* soundtrack."

At last, a tiny smile touched her lips. "You're such a sap, Michael."

"Guilty as charged."

"It could have been me."

"It wasn't."

I rested my hand on her left knee, gently. After a moment, she took my hand and laced our fingers together. We remained quiet for the rest of the time we spent on that swing set, because there was nothing left to say.

WRATH III

"Have I mentioned before that you're weird?"

"Says the guy who eats asparagus raw and can fly."

"…point taken."

"Exactly. Now hush and hand me the vanilla extract."

I reached into the cabinet and passed Jordan the aforementioned tiny brown bottle. She stood in her small split-counter kitchen, her black hair tied back with a blue scarf, leaning over a bowl of cookie dough. Flour dusted her fingers. The faint scent of cinnamon, sugar, and canned pumpkin clung to the air.

She measured the dark liquid in one of those petite metal spoons and poured it into the orange mush in the bottom of the white ceramic bowl. Earlier, she'd been complaining about the lack of sweets in her place, so I ran to the supermarket and bought her the ingredients for, according to her, "the most delicious cookies on the planet." Considering I had traversed the earth in its entirety at certain points in my life, I took her up on the challenge.

Moreover, Jordan rarely cooked. She ate the simplest of meals at home—spaghetti, chicken fingers, tacos, and various soups. I couldn't resist the chance to see her doing something even vaguely domestic. She moved back and forth with smooth, practiced motions, and the ever-present frown on her face was nowhere to be found.

"Where'd you get this recipe anyway?" I asked, stealing another couple of semi-sweet chocolate chips out of the bag.

She swatted my hand as I retracted it and glared. "Mrs. LeBeau gave it to me when I finally moved out of her place. She said they are a surefire way to catch a husband."

I arched an eyebrow. "Is there something you need to tell me, Jordan?"

She rolled her eyes and dumped the rest of the chocolate chips into the cookie mix. "Only in your dreams would I ever consider wooing you, pretty boy."

"No, it's too late," I said, filling my voice with a love-struck tone. I walked up behind her and placed my hands on either side of the counter, trapping her between my arms. "I've fallen for you completely. Your baking skills had me at hello."

She shook her head and didn't bother turning around, merely spooning the cookie dough onto the sheet nearby. "You watch too many movies."

"No such thing."

I dutifully moved aside when she went to place the now-full pan inside the oven and set the timer. "Did you used to cook for him?"

"Who?"

"Your ex."

She glanced at me in surprise and then quickly hid it behind a mask of indifference. "Not really. His aunt was a professional chef, so he knew how to cook way better than I did."

I studied her guarded expression and opened my mouth to apologize for prying, but then someone pounded on the front door. My instincts took over. A couple seconds later, I realized I'd shoved Jordan behind me.

"Calm down, He-Man," she said, but her voice wasn't hard with sarcasm like usual. She patted my arm and went to the door. I trailed behind her, flexing my hands open and closed as fresh adrenaline pumped through my veins. I stretched my spiritual energy outward through the entrance to her apartment. Not a demon or an evil spirit. Good.

Jordan opened the door, revealing a girl who couldn't have been eighteen. She was skinny, had black-and-white streaked hair, a nose ring, and mascara smeared down her cheeks. Her brown eyes were red and puffy with tears. She gave a cry when her gaze fell on me.

"Oh my God, it *is* you!"

She flung herself at me, wrapping her thin arms around my back. I froze.

"What's me?" I asked.

She pulled back and gripped two handfuls of my shirt. "You have to help me. I've done something terrible. It's all my fault!"

"Slow down," I said, resting my hands on her shaking shoulders and pushing her back a couple of steps. "First of all, who are you? Second of all, how do you know me? Third of all, what's your fault?"

"My name is Sarah. I know we've never met before, but I know who you are. You're the archangel Michael."

My confusion quickly switched to suspicion. Jordan shut the door and came to my side, frowning. "Wait, kid. How the hell do you know about the angels?"

"I-I found out from my friends at school. There's this underground conspiracy website that we got a few laughs out of over the past week. It's encoded and we had some fun decrypting until we started hearing about something else. They talked about this man who could make all your dreams come true. All you had to do was call a number and leave your name. He'd find you later and make an offer. I didn't care about it until…"

She let out a hoarse sob. "…until my mom told me we were moving to Florida next month. It's just her and me now that Dad left. My whole life is here, and so are my friends, and I was just so angry that I—"

" — called the man and told him who you were." I finished for her, closing my eyes as the rest of the story began to dawn on me.

"He showed up five minutes later and he promised he could make my mom change her mind. He said that I'd just owe him something in return and he'd make the problem go away. I thought he was just going to talk her out of it, so I agreed."

"What did he do after that?"

The girl pulled down the hem of her jacket, revealing a jagged symbol burned into her right shoulder. It was hellspeak for "branded." "He said he'd go after my mom, and then he'd come back for me. I didn't know what else to do, so I ran and found you."

"How?" Jordan asked. "How did you know where we'd be?"

"That website, they said you were an archangel and that you had this waitress girlfriend who lives here. I panicked. I'm so sorry! I shouldn't have done this. Now he's gonna kill her and I don't know what to do!"

"Sarah, you need to calm down," Jordan said in a level voice. "Sit."

She pushed the teenager down onto her couch and turned to me. "What are you thinking?"

"He's a peddler demon," I said, crossing my arms behind my back and pacing. It helped me think for some reason. "They specialize in tricking desperate souls into giving them what they want. This website has to be recent. There's an entire network of angels devoted to covering up anything related to our existence. Maybe he's getting brazen, or maybe he's trying to lure us out. Either way, it's bad news."

I turned to Sarah. "Describe him."

"Um, he was tall, kind of thin, pale, blond hair, green eyes."

"How long ago did you make the contract?"

"I dunno. Maybe half an hour."

"Where is your mother?"

"She's still at work. She's a telemarketer for a phone company on the west side."

"It'd be too messy to take her out at work," I muttered. "He'd wait until she left."

I raised my voice to Sarah. "Give me your mother's cellphone number."

"It's 518-555-9024."

I faced Jordan. "Stay with her. I'm going after him."

She caught my sleeve. "Michael —"

"I need you here, Jordan," I said, hardening my voice. "If I'm too late, he'll come for her. This place is blessed from top to bottom, but peddler demons can get creative. He'll find a way to get you out of here if he has to burn this apartment to the ground. She needs you more than I do. Keep her safe."

She sighed and nodded. "I will. I promise."

"Have Sarah show you the website and call Gabriel. He should be able to get it taken down."

"Got it."

I offered her a reassuring smile and squeezed her arm. "Save me a cookie."

With that, I hurried out the door to find the conniving bastard hunting Sarah's mother.

It was fifteen minutes to nine o'clock when I arrived at the office building where Sarah's mother worked. One of my buddies at the Albany police department had been kind enough to get me a trace on her phone, confirming she was here.

The parking garage was largely empty by now. Dim lights flickered and buzzed overhead as I walked up to the second level where her car—a beat up green Mazda—sat between a couple others.

The peddler demon leaned against the wall by the elevator connecting the garage to the office building. He wore a navy trench coat over a white V-neck t-shirt and blue jeans. His blond hair was oiled away from a severe face with sharp cheekbones that damn near poked out of his skin. I let him see me approach through the shadows. No need for secrecy. After all, we knew each other.

"Michael," the demon purred, his lips stretching into a grin. "Michael the archangel. How long has it been?"

I came to a stop about five feet away from him and tucked my hands in my pockets. "Six decades, maybe?"

He tracked his jade-green eyes over me from head to toe. "Yes, I remember now. Your hair was shorter and you had a beard."

He plucked the cig from his lips with those bony fingers and blew out a stream of smoke. "So how have you been?"

I shrugged. "Not bad."

"I'll bet," he said with a smirk. "Word on the street is that you've shacked up with a Seer. They say she's sweet as a Hershey's kiss. I'm surprised you didn't bring her along."

"She's a bit busy at the moment, cleaning up one of your messes."

He laid a hand on his chest. "*Moi?* Why, what have I done now?

I let the feigned civility bleed out of my expression, leaving it cold. "I believe you met a girl named Sarah tonight."

"Ah, yes. How is the little dear?"

"She came to me for help."

"Whatever would she need that for?"

"Cut the shit, Shylock. She didn't know any better."

He shrugged. "And that is my problem how?"

"You're not going to kill a child's mother. Not while I'm still breathing. Not in my town."

Shylock laughed. The sound bore similarities to having lumps of coal shoved into my eardrums. "So this is your turf now, Michael? Are you telling me to step off?"

"I haven't been involved in the business of preventing soul-trafficking for a while now, but this is different. There used to be rules. You and your kind stayed away from kids. What happened? Are people getting wise to you now? Are your numbers in Hell down or something?"

He shook his head. "It was an opportunity. I took advantage. Quick, clean, and easy. I didn't think she'd go looking for help."

I stepped forward, taking my hands out of my pockets and balling them into fists. "The hell you didn't. The only way she knew you were going to kill her mother is that you told her. You wanted her scared. You wanted her miserable. You used to have an honor code."

"Times have changed, Mike. And, by the way, if you want to blame someone, blame yourself."

"What?" I snarled in disbelief.

He flicked the cigarette to the ground and glared at me. "Do you know how many souls I was promised when Belial revealed that he was going to inhabit your body and take over? Thousands, maybe even millions. I'm not a free agent. I have a quota of souls to deliver or my ass gets thrown back to the Pit. Then you and your little girlfriend ruined it, and now I'm screwed. I'll take what I can get, and I don't care how."

His story made sense, at the very least. Peddler demons tended to be low on the power pyramid. He really didn't have a choice. "I don't care about your byline. Let the girl go."

Shylock spread his hands and the defensive anger vanished like magic. "Sorry, mate. It's a verbal contract. You can bully me all you like, but it's not getting nullified."

At last, I allowed the humorless smile building inside me to spread across my mouth. "Oh, I'm not going to bully you. You know me better than that."

"I do."

"Since you knew about Belial's scheme, then you must also know that we are in possession of the Spear of Longinus, right?"

The first sign of uneasiness touched his features. He frowned. "Yeah, so?"

"So you know that it has the ability to displace a soul from one's body."

"And?"

"And if you don't release Sarah from the contract, I'm going to eject your piddling little soul from your body and throw your ass in Purgatory."

His gemstone eyes widened. "You're bluffing."

I pushed my duster aside, reaching for the small of my back like I was going to pull a weapon. "Am I? You sure? You want to bet your eternal existence on it?"

He swallowed hard. "Come on, man. I'm just doing my job. She's the one to blame."

"You shouldn't be thinking about her," I murmured, stalking even closer. "You can't collect any souls if you're no longer on earth. Think about it. Floating in a void for years, decades, centuries, with no power. Nothing to manipulate. No bargains to make. No sins to commit. Just you and an endless space until Judgment Day. Is that what you want?"

His gaze darted between my face and my arm, still poised behind me like I was going to pull out the Spear. Tense silence filled the air between us.

Then the elevator dinged.

"Shit!" the demon exclaimed. "Fine! I release Sarah Whitman from her contract. You have my word as a demon."

I lowered my arm and stepped away. "Smart man."

Seconds later, the elevator doors opened. A woman in her late thirties with messy hair and bags under her eyes walked out. The shape of her nose and the brown of her eyes were a dead ringer for Sarah. She cast a suspicious glare over the two of us and then hurried to her car.

I waited until she was out of earshot before addressing the demon again. "Stay away from the kids, Shy. This is my only warning."

He spat at my feet. "You're still a goddamn bully, after all this time."

I smirked. "And you're still chickenshit."

He snorted and fumbled for another cigarette. "Beat it, archangel."

I turned and headed back the way I came, though after making sure Sarah's mother drove away without her car exploding or something equally unfortunate.

Jordan and Sarah were sitting on the couch when I returned — the former with her arm around the latter's shoulders. I'd called ahead to let them know Sarah's mother was safe, and Jordan confirmed that the brand on Sarah's arm had disappeared. Still, my job was only half done.

"Thank you so much," the girl said after I'd closed the door. "I can't repay you for this."

"You can and you will," I said, narrowing my eyes at her. "Do you have *any* idea how wrong it could have gone tonight? Do you understand what would have happened if I hadn't gotten you out of that contract? Your mother would have gotten stabbed and died alone, bleeding out in a parking lot, and your soul would burn in Hell for all eternity."

"I'm sorry—"

"Sorry isn't good enough. You were reckless. You endangered yourself and the person most important to you. She raised you. I don't care if she's not doing as good a job as you'd like. She's your mother. You only get one, and some people aren't that lucky."

Fresh tears spilled down her cheeks. "I'll do anything to make it up, please."

I crossed my arms. "Go home. Make your mother dinner. Tell her you're sorry and you'll do anything that she asks. Make damn sure she knows you appreciate everything that she does for you. As for your friends, don't ever let them talk you into something so stupid ever again. Find people who truly care about you and spend the rest of your life learning from this mistake. Then we'll be even. Got it?"

She nodded too many times. "I will. I promise."

She stood. Jordan did too. "I'll walk her home."

"Good. Watch your back."

They disappeared out the door. A huge sigh of relief escaped me. I didn't like playing bad cop in these situations, but it was necessary. Teenagers often needed to be scared straight. I'd been harsh enough that she would probably stay on the righteous path. I could only hope so, if she and others like her were the future.

By the time Jordan returned, I had spoken with the angels responsible for monitoring the proof of our existence. The site was already down, and so were any forums connected to it. Good. We had enough problems anyway.

"So," Jordan said, tossing her grey duster on the couch next to me. "That was an adventure."

I ran my hands through my hair and dragged them down the length of my face. Stubble greeted my fingertips. Needed to shave in the morning. "Understatement of the year."

"Not the century?"

I raised an eyebrow. "You've met me, right?"

She chuckled. "Point taken. You poured it on pretty hard. She kept telling me the whole way to apologize again for her. She thinks you hate her."

"Necessary evil. She probably wasn't even a bad kid. I'll never understand how teenagers can do things like that without thinking."

"It's human nature. We identify what is best for us and then immediately do the opposite. The more time you spend down here, the more you'll realize I'm right."

"Sad, but probably true."

"It's not all bad, though."

"How so?"

Jordan smiled and went into the kitchen. She came back with a glass of milk, and two pumpkin chocolate chip cookies neatly wrapped in a napkin. "Cookies are done."

"Marry me." I accepted the offerings and tipped the glass in her direction. After my night, I'd earned it.

I sipped the milk and then bit into one of the cookies. "…holy *shit*."

PRIDE

We only tried grappling once.

Jordan was five-foot-six, so odds were her opponents would be taller and broader than her. Her personal trainer and mentor, Jared, had gotten busier with clients toward the fall season, and she needed help now that she'd caught the demons' attention. I offered to teach her some good takedowns to help with her functional but limited self-defense techniques. She still lived alone, and I wouldn't be at her side forever. I'd sleep better knowing she could fight both the supernatural and the natural scumbags of the world.

"Alright," I said after we both finished stretching. After some extensive searching, we found a spot in the back of the gym with enough space to practice away from prying eyes. "I'll start with the basics. I'm sure Jared's told you the best thing for girls your size is to use your opponent's weight and size against them. It means fewer hits for you to take and you have a better chance of coming out on top."

She placed one hand on her slender hip and arched an eyebrow. "We're not about to reenact that scene from *Miss Congeniality* where Gracie kicks Eric's ass in front of everyone, are we?"

"Are you kidding? You're nowhere near as dreamy as Benjamin Bratt."

She rolled her eyes. "My mistake. Continue."

"If you get caught, your first instinct might be to panic. Don't. That's exactly how you lose. You're pretty good about staying cool under pressure, but I have to mention it anyway just to be thorough. Control your breathing and analyze the situation."

I held my hands shoulder width apart. "So you already know the best thing during an attack is to head for the soft targets—eyes, ears, mouth, nose, groin, fingers, and toes—but what I want to focus on is close quarters bumrush attacks. You're fast and you know what to look for, but you wouldn't be able to keep up with a demon. That means you'll have to think fast instead."

I stepped in close and hunched my shoulders. "Guys are simple. They think like bulls—head down, body weight in full force. You can use this to your advantage. Wait until they're at about a foot away and aim for the face with your elbow. Hit upward hard. It'll either knock them away or daze them so they can't concentrate on hurting you if you both fall. Ready?"

She sent me a worried look. "You want me to hit you in the nose with my elbow?"

"Not exactly. I'm gonna hold my hand out at the spot you need to hit. I'd rather not accidentally bite my tongue in half."

"That I could live with," she said without hesitation. "But I'd better not mark up that pretty face of yours or someone will call the cops on me."

"Talk shit *after* you've stopped me."

She scowled but adopted the defensive stance she knew already—sideways, with her fists raised at about shoulder level, her feet planted apart, and her chin up. I backtracked about seven steps and reminded myself not to apply all of my strength or I'd knock her through the wall.

A handful of tense seconds slipped by. Her alert brown eyes tracked over me, waiting for my attack. Loose strands of raven hair escaped her ever-present high ponytail and settled against her left cheek.

I rushed her. She reacted with a graceful kind of fluidity, but I managed to get one hand on her shoulder before her elbow hit my palm.

I cocked my head to the left. "See what I meant? You hesitated."

She shook off my hand. "I did not. You're just faster than I thought."

"Is this the part where I say 'that's what she said'?"

"Shut up and do it again, pretty boy."

I came at her a second time. She swung at me, faster, harder, and I could tell the hit would have connected if I stayed the course. I ducked so that her arm went over my head and then came up behind her. In seconds, I locked her into a full nelson.

"This is something else to consider," I said. "The untrained bad guy might fall for the elbow shot, but the smart ones might put you into something like this."

"Comfy," Jordan said through her teeth. She didn't struggle, but she couldn't help wiggling a little with my arms around her shoulders. It was a bit distracting.

"So how the hell do I get out of this one, *sensei*?"

"It's a bit difficult, but not impossible. Stomp on the toes or in-step and nine times out of ten, they'll let go enough for you to get out. If they don't grip your neck—" I moved my palm aside so she could feel the difference. " — you can try for a head butt. It hurts like a son of a bitch, but the top of your skull is way thicker than the bones in his nose."

"Any other way out?"

"If you're in one of these with a pro, you might be S.O.L, but you can go limp quickly and yank your arms free when they're completely straight. You're on the skinny side so they might lose their grip."

The second after I spoke, she did just that—let her weight drop her close to the floor and then slipped out of my grip. She smirked, placing her hands on her hips.

"Not bad for a human, huh?"

And there it was. The focal point of our little training session. I relaxed my body and smiled. "Perfect."

Then I tripped her and pinned her to the mat.

She had good enough reflexes to catch herself on her hands, but I was at least five times faster than her, and that was being modest. I anchored her wrists to the floor on either side of her head and straddled her waist, though I didn't put any weight down. She struggled for a few seconds, tugging at her arms to no avail, and then let her head drop onto the mat with an exasperated sigh.

"I suppose I walked right into that one."

I shrugged. "Expect the unexpected and all that jazz."

She frowned. "Please, be *more* condescending."

My fingers tightened their grip on her wrists. "It's hard not to be, with your ego in the way."

"My *ego*?" she spat. "I've managed to stay alive by myself for twenty-one years."

"We're playing a different ball game now, Jordan. Tell me you see that."

"Of course I do." She tried to push up from the ground with her legs, but I didn't budge. The movement arched her entire lithe form. She was wearing basketball shorts and a tank top. It wasn't difficult to notice certain…*attributes*…of hers. Lust threatened to emerge from the depths where I'd stuffed it down. *Focus, Michael.*

A frustrated growl spilled out of her throat after she couldn't get free. "Why do you think I went behind your back and got lessons from Jared?"

"Why didn't you just ask me?"

"Because of *this*." She twisted her arms to emphasize the way I'd pinned her. "You make me feel like I don't know anything. Like I'm helpless. I'm not a damsel in distress. I can fight. I can take care of myself."

"No one said you couldn't, but you're overestimating your abilities—"

"—and you're underestimating my abilities just because you're an archangel, so we're even."

I stared into those angry brown eyes until her words seeped in. *I'm not a damsel in distress.* I thought of how I'd found her the night Belial attacked—handcuffed, hanging there with blood soaking her shirt, unable to stop the archdemon from completing his nefarious work. Alone.

"You're right," I said. "Maybe we're both at fault. I'm not trying to make you feel helpless, Jordan. I'm trying to make sure you live to see retirement age, and you can't do that without humbling yourself. I know you're strong. But they don't. If they come for you and you're not ready, then everything you've fought for won't matter. I don't know how long I'll be here, but until I find out, you have to let me help you. Can you do that?"

The stubborn frown stayed firmly rooted on her face at first, but then she sighed in resignation. "Fine. Now unless you're buying me dinner, get off."

I arched an eyebrow. "You let your dates put you in full body pins?"

She gave me a catty smirk. "Who said anything about let?"

The comment was distracting enough that I lost a couple seconds thanks to my overactive imagination. Before I knew it, we had rolled and she was on top of me. She didn't try to pin my arms. She just sat snugly across my lower stomach, grinning.

"You're not the only one with moves, Mr. O'Brien."

"Clearly," I said. It came out huskier than I'd intended. We were both breathing heavy by now and in sync somehow. I didn't recall being in this situation before, with a pretty girl in my lap. I liked it far more than I should have — the upward tilt of her plump lips, the thin sheen of sweat that made her brown skin glow under the fluorescent lights, the rise and fall of her breasts, the warmth of her toned thighs on either side of my hips, and the playfulness glinting in those dark eyes.

A loud wolf whistle cut through the air, distracting us both. I turned my head to see Jordan's best friend, Lauren Yi, standing a few feet away in yoga pants and a red cut off t-shirt. She had a mat tucked under her arm. A group of women filed out of the room across from us, giving Jordan and me appreciative looks when they passed by.

"Well, well," the Korean girl purred. "Doesn't this look friendly?"

Jordan glared. "He was teaching me how to wrestle."

Lauren's eyes slid to the infinite lack of space between our pelvises. "I bet he was."

Jordan heaved herself off me and offered her hand. I took it and she pulled me up.

Lauren raised her hand. "I got next."

"I'm so going to hurt you," Jordan growled.

Lauren pouted. "Oh, sure. Keep the hunk all to yourself. I see how it is."

"Don't encourage him," Jordan said, grabbing her water bottle from where it rested at the corner of the mat. "Do you know how long it took us to find this spot? Like twenty minutes, because every single girl in this joint flirted with him on the way."

I crossed my arms. "Hey, it's not my fault some women actually appreciate me."

"Yeah, until you open your mouth."

"I think we both have that in common—ow!" I rubbed where she'd hit me in the shoulder.

Lauren shook her head. "I give it another month and you two will be at each other like Beatrice and Benedick. Just make sure you send me a card expressing that I was right. I also accept gift certificates. Or if you have a daughter, name her after me."

Jordan massaged her temples. "Good*bye*, Lauren."

She laughed and gave Jordan a one-armed hug. "Lighten up, Jor. See you guys later. Be good. Or don't. I'm fine with either."

She headed towards the locker room to change. As soon as she was out of earshot, Jordan's annoyance melted into genuine concern. "Sorry. She's...got an abrasive sort of personality. It also helps that I haven't had a guy for a friend in a really long time so she goes overboard on the jokes."

"It's fine," I assured her, running my small towel across the back of my neck to mop up the sweat. "I can see how she'd misinterpret our relationship. She means well. She just wants you to be happy."

"Don't know if you're up for that," she said, and her tone was a bit sad. "But I'll stick with prepared for now."

I bumped her shoulder with mine. "Being happy and being prepared are not mutually exclusive. Cheer up, Amador. You've got time. I promise."

She smiled. It was one of those rare ones with no sarcasm or cynicism in it. The light from the smile touched every curve of her face. It was...beautiful.

I cleared my throat when I realized I'd been staring. "How about a snack? My treat?"

She nodded. "Lead the way."

We went to the vending machines and ended up wasting the rest of the session eating chocolate covered granola bars and talking about our least favorite health foods. And that worked for me just fine.

PRIDE II

"Stop hogging it."

"I'm not hogging it."

"You are. I've only had two and you've already had five."

Jordan's bottom lip pushed outward, a childish gesture. I doubt she noticed she did that when she scowled, but I always did. "Why are you even counting?"

"That's beside the point. Hand it over."

She cradled the small plastic container of caramel dip to her chest, the other gripping the Tupperware full of sliced green apples with unmatched ferocity. I had underestimated this girl's lust for sweets. She was getting stingy.

"I did not have five! I had…four and a half."

"Uh-huh." I rolled my eyes, reaching across the couch and snatching an apple slice before she could jerk it away. I dipped it in the caramel and ate it, tossing her a petulant look.

"Well, it's only fair," she harrumphed. "I bought it."

"Yeah, with that five-dollar bill I gave you last week."

"Lies and garbage. That was my five," she replied through another mouthful of fruit. Gabriel had once called her stubborn. Ha. Understatement of the century. And I would know.

"Really? You're gonna lie to an archangel?" I asked, cocking an eyebrow upward.

"Not lying. You're remembering it wrong."

"Oh, so now I have a faulty memory? That's it."

She tossed me a skeptical look. "What's it?"

"You have lost your sweets privileges. Gimme." I reached for them, stretching across the couch to reach. I was of course kidding, but I let my voice sound completely deadpan just to mess with her.

"No way!" She stuck her socked foot out against my chest, holding me off. I grinned and instead dug my fingers into her sides. She burst into laughter, squirming.

"S-Stop it, you son of a—"

"Then quit boggarting the caramel."

She wiggled free and dipped a slice in the caramel, holding it out to me as a peace offering. "Here, here! Take it, you monster!"

I caught her wrist and ate the piece in one bite, smirking in victory. To add insult to injury, I licked the rest of the caramel off of her fingers, which made her giggle even harder than before.

"Ugh, quit it, Lord knows where your mouth has been," she groaned.

"It's probably cleaner than yours," I said, somehow oddly fixated on how dainty her digits were. There was still a glob of the delicious treat on her pinky so I sucked it clean without thinking. It was then that I noticed she had stopped giggling and she was staring up at me with a look I couldn't quite classify in my brain. Then again, it seemed like we were both breathing a little heavier than before too. What had changed?

I kept telling myself to let go of her, but for some reason my mouth was still on her ring finger and it seemed to no longer have anything to do with caramel. It didn't help that she was lying underneath me in just a large t-shirt and shorts. Her golden brown legs looked endless. Sometime during our fooling around, her ponytail had come loose and her hair framed her cheeks. And then there was the fact that she hadn't pulled her hand away, or even tried to, since I started sucking her fingertips.

At some point, I had the presence of mind to let go of her wrist, but she still didn't lower her hand, instead settling it on the side of my chin. I could definitely feel it now. We were both breathing hard and the couch suddenly felt entirely too small for comfort.

I didn't remember leaning down. It just happened. One minute we were staring at each other and the next my breath was cascading down one side of her cheek and my mind floated off into the ether, wondering if I'd be able to taste the caramel apples on her tongue. She shifted upward and her nose grazed mine, her body close enough that her knees brushed either side of my hips. She laid her hand on my chest. All the oxygen in the room seemed to vanish at once. I was seconds away from drowning in her.

Then she cleared her throat and pushed against my upper body, separating us. She said my name once, softly, but in that measured tone I heard a warning and remembered who and what I was like a bolt of lightning. *Shit.*

"Jordan, I—"

She shook her head. "It's okay. Happens."

I nodded, but I don't think either of us believed her. "It's late. I'd better head out. Got work in the morning."

"Mmkay. Night, Michael."

"Night, Jordan."

I stood, unable to meet her eyes. Then again, she wasn't really trying to catch my gaze. I'd read about this somewhere. They called it a near miss. I was too proud to apologize and she was too proud to admit she'd been tempted. Maybe we were just fooling ourselves into thinking we could make this work.

I had my hand on the doorknob when she called out to me. "Hey."

I froze, tilting my head enough to see her. She pushed her hair out of her face, seeming young and vulnerable in the faint light from the television.

"See you tomorrow?"

Relief spread through my chest. "Yeah. See you tomorrow."

God help us both.

PRIDE III

My name is Michael O'Brien.

I am an archangel.

I can punch a hole through a mountain.

I can run fast enough to make Barry Allen blush.

I can fight thirty maniacal demons at once with my bare hands.

I can hold my breath underwater for up to eighty minutes.

But for some damn reason, I cannot beat Jordan frickin' Amador at Tekken 6.

"This game is cheating."

Jordan cackled, her thumbs hammering on the buttons of the controller. "The game is not cheating."

"It is," I insisted. My anger swelled as the life bar to my leopard-masked wrestler got lower and lower every time Jordan's impossibly fast Chinese martial artist hit him. "It can't register how fast I'm hitting these buttons."

"So, wait," she said through another bout of sadistic giggles. "You're cheating and using your powers…and you're *still* losing?"

I gritted my teeth. "That is irrelevant. The controller is broken."

"The controller is not broken."

To add insult to injury, she performed an elegant final takedown and the match ended. I'd lost for the eighth time tonight. I palmed my face with both hands, resisting the urge to break the PlayStation 3 into a thousand tiny pieces and then set them on fire.

Jordan poked me in the side with her socked foot. "You okay over there?"

"Don't touch me."

She laughed harder. "Michael, you are a celestial being of untold grace and power. How is it you're this much of a sore loser?"

I dropped my hands and glared at her. "Because this is just sad. I can literally pick up an elephant with one hand. I've been to the bottom of the Pacific Ocean. I've been to *Mars*, for shit's sake! So why in the hell can't I beat you?"

She shook her head. "It has nothing to do with your abilities as an angel. It's all technique."

"What technique? I know literally every style of martial arts known to mankind. I'm the Batman of the supernatural world, damn it. Remember that time Satan waged war in Heaven and I saved the entire universe from evil?"

"Your ego is literally going to blow a crater in Albany right now."

I ground my back teeth. "You're a girl. You don't get it. It's a guy thing."

Jordan rolled her eyes and took a sip of her soda. "Don't tell me you believe in that bullshit nonsense that all guys are better than girls at video games."

"Of course not. It's just irking me that you have no discernible attack plan and yet you're wiping the floor with me."

She arched an eyebrow. "Did it ever occur to you that you're losing for that exact reason?"

"How so?"

"You're over-thinking it. You're not applying for MENSA. You're just playing a game. It's for fun. Remember that thing called fun?"

I crossed my arms, scowling. "It's only fun because you're winning."

"Alright, you giant man-baby, then maybe we should try something else."

"No. I'm not quitting until I win."

She checked her watch. "You do realize it's almost three in the morning."

I picked up my controller. "So?"

"Why should I keep playing with your stubborn ass?"

"Because if I lose this next match, I'll sleep on the couch, you get my bed, and I'll make you breakfast in the morning."

"...you're on."

Five minutes later…

"…damn it, Jordan!"

GREED

"So."

"So."

Lauren Yi's smoky brown eyes studied me as if there were nothing else interesting in the room, despite the fact that I was pretty sure the dude in the corner had just dropped some acid and there were two girls in cat suits making out by the bar. Then again, she'd suggested coming to this club, so maybe that was normal.

She was a direct contrast in appearance to Jordan — taller, curvier, and certainly girlier. She wore a blood-orange dress with a plunging neckline, platform heels that almost made her my height, a handful of gold bracelets on each arm, and big hoop earrings that glittered under her long black hair. We hadn't known each other long, but I could tell Lauren enjoyed being seen. Couldn't blame her. She was a knockout.

"You and Jordan have been hanging out a lot these days."

"Yeah," I said, trying to sound casual over the pounding techno music. "It's been fun."

She swirled the red straw in her Long Island iced tea, still staring at me. "So are you two boffing or what?"

I couldn't hide the surprise on my face. I'd heard she was blunt, but this was ridiculous. "No, we're just friends. Why do you ask?"

Lauren shrugged. "To be honest, I hardly see Jordan except at work because she's always with you. You put a man and a woman together that long and something's bound to happen."

I shook my head. "No. If we were together, you'd know. I'm not the kind of guy who'd lie about something like that."

She arched a thin eyebrow. "Really? Like you lied about being her at-home assistant?"

I opened my mouth to deny it, but she shook her head. "Don't insult my intelligence. I checked. No one at that hospital has even heard of you."

"Do you always check people's backgrounds?"

"Only when they're hanging out at my best friend's apartment at all hours of the night."

"Fair enough."

A glint of something flashed through her eyes. Suspicion, maybe. "Why aren't you dating her, then?"

I licked my bottom lip, trying to buy myself a couple of seconds to think. Lauren, sweet girl that she was, knew nothing about the world of angels and demons, and it was my job to keep it that way.

"I guess it's just a chemistry thing. I could spend all day with Jordan, but I just don't think about her that way. She's sorta like—"

Lauren waved her hand. "If you say she's like your sister, I will smack you. I've seen you two interact. Jordan and Gabriel are like siblings. You two aren't. Try again, Mr. O'Brien."

She was definitely a bright girl. No wonder Jordan liked her so much. Finally, I just smiled at her. "It's complicated. Does that help?"

She flashed me a grin. "That's the most honest thing you've said all night, handsome."

I chuckled. "Thanks."

Someone tapped me on the shoulder. I turned my head to see a pretty blonde in a royal purple dress. She tossed her curly hair over one shoulder and gave me a big smile.

"Hey there. Wanna dance?"

I shook my head and gestured between myself and Lauren. "We're waiting for someone. Maybe later?"

She pouted, but walked off just the same. I turned around to see Lauren's grin even wider.

"Wow. That's, what? Six girls in a row? Does this always happen when you go out?"

"Not sure. I don't pay much attention."

She propped her chin up on her hand. "Okay, now I'm curious. What's your type? Not one of those girls made you even think twice about getting up."

I shrugged. "Don't really have a type."

"I'd almost think you were gay, but I have caught you glancing down my dress once or twice."

I cleared my throat. Heat rushed up my neck and filtered into my cheeks. "Sorry."

She laughed. "No harm done. Seriously, though, what are you looking for in a woman?"

I hesitated. It had previously occurred to me that Lauren might fancy me, and I definitely didn't want to inadvertently cause tension between her and Jordan. Then again, it wasn't like Jordan was going out with me, so it wouldn't be an issue on her part. I wasn't allowed to date anyone as an archangel, human or Seer.

In the end, I went for the vague answer. "I suppose I'll know it when I see it. What about you? I've seen you look around, but no one seems to be grabbing your attention either."

She sipped her tea before answering. "I'm not in the mood for guys yet. Hence the alcohol. There's a bit of potential in this crowd, but I'm not looking to take anyone home tonight. Jordan and I usually come here to get social, not much else. Have you gone dancing with her before?"

"No. I got the impression she didn't want me along, but she didn't want to be rude when you asked me to come with you two."

She patted the back of my hand. "Don't take it personal. She's just insecure about her dancing skills. I've had to work at getting her comfortable with her own body."

She paused. "That sounded a lot more sexual than I intended."

"No complaints here."

Lauren pursed her lips. "Men. You're all perverts, I swear."

"Hey, just being honest."

Lauren raised her drink. "Can't argue with that. To honesty."

I mirrored her, clinking our glasses together. "To honesty."

As if on cue, Jordan returned from the bathroom and slid into the booth next to her best friend. Jordan's clubbing attire was much subtler than Lauren's—a simple dress that was white from the waist up and black at the waist down, silver jewelry, and low heels. Her black hair was pulled back into a French bun. She had a bit of bluish-silver eye-shadow on and clear lip gloss to finish the look. The overall effect was quite stunning.

"Hey," Jordan said. "What'd I miss?"

"We were just discussing the sexual tension between you two," Lauren supplied. I spat out my drink and fell into a violent bout of coughing.

Jordan shook her head. "See, this is why I can't take you anywhere."

"Whatever, you love me," Lauren said breezily. "Now come on, we've been sitting here all night. Let's dance."

The two ladies scooted out of the booth. I stayed put, intending to finish my pint of Yuengling beer, but then Lauren stopped on her way to the dance floor. "Uh, what are you doing, Stilts?"

I glanced at her. "What?"

"You're coming with."

I frowned. "I was under the impression I'm only supposed to leave the booth if some guy tries to get fresh. I don't dance."

Lauren rolled her eyes and marched back over to me. "First of all, what century were you born in? No one says 'get fresh' anymore. Second of all, no one goes to a club and stays in the booth the whole time on my watch. Up and at 'em, boy-toy."

She grabbed my wrist and tugged until I groaned and vacated my seat. "Fine. One dance."

Truth be told, I was lying. I could dance, just not the way these people were. I'd had a few missions in the past where I'd impersonated a gentleman at a party for surveillance purposes. I knew most of the traditional dances — ballroom, the waltz, the tango — but the modern equivalent of dancing baffled me. It was basically just upright dry humping.

Bright red and blue lights jolted from the ceiling onto random spots of the dance floor, illuminating the crowd of twenty-somethings. The club itself had two levels — the main bottom floor where the bar was and an upper floor with couches, tables, and chairs. The DJ was on a platform at the far wall, occasionally grabbing the mic to ask the patrons if they were having a good time.

We were on the fringe of the dance floor when I felt my pocket vibrating. I stopped and checked my phone. Gabriel was calling. He usually only called when it involved a case — anything else between us was texting. I motioned to Lauren that I had a call to take and she frowned, but let me go.

I hurried in the direction of the men's room and answered once the door closed behind me. There were a couple guys at the urinals, but by the sound of it, they'd had a few drinks. Wouldn't matter if they overheard my conversation.

"Hey, Gabe. What's up?"

"I've got an update for you on the hellhound killings."

Immediately, my mood sobered. "Go on."

"We finally isolated a common factor between the six victims. They all had various backgrounds and financial standings, but over the past couple years, each of them has worked with Lanning and Holmes. It's a law firm on the east side."

"Past clients?"

"Looks to be that way. It's clear that someone in their office is involved."

"Did you get a name?"

"It is not just one person. Based on the information I gathered, the victims saw different people."

"Who is in charge of the firm?"

"Jean Winters." The rareness of his first name — pronounced the French way, like Jean Claude Van Damme — stuck out to me.

"Winters," I muttered, running a hand through my hair. "Why does that name sound familiar?"

"I thought so too. Do you remember working a case with me in the late '70's? We were deployed in Atlanta, tracking down several slayings with a similar M.O?"

"Yeah. We found the underlings, but not the guy who ran the operation. If I recall correctly, he was targeting the accounts of loners and systematically acquiring their wealth, since the animal attacks were always passed off as random. Was that Winters?"

"We never got a first name, but it is possible this demon is the same one."

"Then kicking his ass is way overdue."

"Indeed. What are your thoughts?"

I checked my watch. "It's half-past eleven now, so there's probably no one at his office. Start checking his social circles and financial statements for the past year. I'll go around town and see if I can pick up on the hellhound's trail."

"Will do. Be careful, brother. This hound has killed six people. It is clearly not your average predator."

I smiled before I could help myself. Centuries of working together and he still worried about me like I was his kid brother. "I'll be fine. I'll call you when I've got something."

"Good luck."

I hung up and headed out the door. The wall of dance music smashed into me as soon as I left the bathroom. I wove through the ever-increasing crowds of people until I reached the dance floor again. The flashing lights and artificial smoke made it hard as hell to see anything, but Lauren's unique dress color finally caught my eye.

She and Jordan were dancing with each other near the stage. The DJ had switched to a reggae song with a frantic beat. Their bodies moved in sensual tandem, hips rocking back and forth, arms thrown in the air, their painted lips wide with smiles. I forgot that Jordan could lead a semi-normal life from time to time. She looked adorable and lively. I almost regretted having to leave.

I made a path through to them and leaned in towards Jordan's right ear. "I've got to take care of a case. I'll probably be late, so you should catch a cab with Lauren back to your place tonight."

"It's not the hellhound attacks, is it?"

"Yeah, why?"

"I want in on that one. One of the girls it killed was a regular at my restaurant."

I frowned. "Jordan, it's going to be dangerous. I don't want to put you in harm's way."

She poked me in the stomach. "I'm always in harm's way. Don't be such a girl."

Before I could say anything else, she tugged Lauren aside and said something in her ear. She nodded and Jordan motioned towards the exit. I sighed and followed them outside of the club into the cold autumn night. I held out my hand and whistled for the nearest cab. The girls waited on the curb behind me.

"I'll make it up to you," Jordan said. "I promise."

"Oh, shush. The club's not going anywhere. We can go out another night, provided that you don't ditch me to bone your hot boyfriend again."

I heard a small slap as if she'd hit Lauren. "He's not my boyfriend."

"I notice you didn't deny the boning part. Ow!"

"Could you stop?"

"Could you take a joke?"

"Maybe if you didn't say stuff like that while he's standing *right there.*"

"He knows I'm kidding, relax."

Mercifully, a cab pulled up alongside me and I opened the door. Lauren slipped in first, Jordan climbed in after her, and I got in last. We dropped Lauren off at her place and then I gave the driver the address to the last victim's apartment.

She was a real estate broker by the name of Lacey Brooks. The apartment was on the south side of Albany. The super found her body in the laundromat on the bottom floor, torn to pieces. We'd connected it to the other killings since the bite marks were too large for any stray dogs in the area, and there were no other similar incidents reported that month. The unusual nature of her death suggested that she was a target.

I got out first and stared up at the building. Faded brick walls. White wooden windows. Mostly occupied by blue collar workers. No cameras or doorman. Very easy access to the tenants.

"When did the attack happen?" Jordan asked, shutting the door to the cab.

"Two days ago," I answered. "No other reports of animal attacks on this side of town. The guy we're chasing did something like this forty years ago."

"It's smart. After all, there's no way any regular person could bring down a hellhound without killing it, meaning there'd be no evidence. The cops would never suspect it was being used as an assassin because it sounds insane. Obviously, the crime scene is off-limits, so what are we looking for?"

"Hounds are sentient, but they still retain the traits of a normal dog," I told her, walking towards the rear of the apartment complex. It was late enough now that the only people outside were a couple shifty-looking teenagers smoking and sitting out by their respective cars. Jordan's heels clicked on the concrete as we went past. One of them whistled at her and she flipped him off. I hid a grin.

"It's still got to eat, drink water, and sleep when it's not on the prowl," I continued. "Winters is too smart to let the animal stay with him. I'm guessing he set it up with some sort of den. I've got Gabriel checking his financials to see if anything corresponds with this area."

"So we're looking for overturned garbage cans and piles of poo?"

"More or less."

She sighed. "We lead such a glamorous life."

"You wanted the ride-along."

"That I did." She took the pins out of her hair and shook it loose as we reached the giant green dumpster at the end of the street. Lauren had talked her out of wearing her usual oversized grey duster she inherited from a past Seer, so she had a slimming black coat instead. Even when she went out for leisure, I'd instructed her to keep a rosary and holy water on her at all times. The vials clinked together in her pocket as she moved around to the other side of the dumpster.

The cold air kept the rotten stench of spoiled food to a minimum, but I still breathed through my mouth as I stepped around the torn plastic bags of garbage. The trash company was due to pick it up in the morning. Good thing we came by tonight.

"I've got some claw marks on this side," Jordan said. "Muddy ones."

"Yeah, they start over here," I replied. "Looks like he couldn't get the door unjammed and tried the other one. Started tearing it up and eating whatever he found until he was full."

Jordan came around the dumpster, pointing at the faint dirt stains leading away to the cluster of trees and yard that separated this complex from the next one. "There's no blood here. He ate first and then attacked her. What did they find at the crime scene?"

"Based on what I saw in the photos, the blood trail leads to the pool area. The damn thing jumped in to clean himself off and then left."

She shook her head. "That just ain't right."

"Tell me about it. Let's go."

"Where are we heading?"

"The closest wooded area to here is Kenwood Academy's estate. Good place to hide, especially at night."

"If we're going into the woods, I definitely need to change."

I glanced back at her as we returned to the curb where the cab had dropped us off. "Or you could just go home."

She crossed her arms and avoided my gaze, scowling. "You're sick of me already? That must be a record."

I lifted my eyes to the heavens. *Women.* "This creature tore out a woman's throat and busted her chest cavity open like a piñata. I don't like the thought of it being anywhere near you."

"Did it ever occur to you that I feel the same way?"

Surprise flooded over me. "No, it...actually didn't."

"I know I'm not as strong or as smart as you are, but that doesn't mean I can't help. We're partners, aren't we?"

"Yeah," I said, and couldn't stop the smile creeping across my lips. "I guess we are."

She tossed a quick look at me and frowned. "Quit it."

"What?"

"I hate it when you do that."

"You hate it when I smile?"

"No, when you make that, 'aw, she does have a heart' face. You look like a Disney prince."

I laughed. "My bad. I'll work on that."

We caught the bus to a 24-hour supermarket nearby. Jordan bought some loose-fitting blue jeans, boots, and a black wool-knit sweater. I bought us a pair of flashlights and gave her my back up knife that I always kept in the lining of my jacket.

Being in the woods at night was never one of my favorite experiences on earth. My military training took over and I knew what to listen for, but it didn't mean I liked it. It was past midnight. Darkness laid over everything like a stifling blanket. The forest had its own soundtrack. Crickets. Owls and other birds of prey. Small lizards and bugs scuttling through the underbrush. The wind whispering sweet nothings to the branches and leaves of the trees. Perfect place for a predator to settle.

Jordan stood to my right with her flashlight in hand. She stayed perfectly still, as if waiting for my cue to follow me into the forest. "Why do I feel like we're about to reenact that scene from *Jurassic Park* with the velociraptors and that Australian hunter guy?"

"Because you watch too many movies," I said, scanning the immediate area for any signs of the hound's trail. "And because this is kind of similar."

"That's comforting."

"You asked." I motioned the beam of light towards the faint line in the dirt and the crushed twigs to our left. "This is a good place to start. Stay close and let me know if you see or hear anything. I've got eyes on front, so watch my back."

"With gusto," she muttered, and then we disappeared into the darkness.

I stretched out my spiritual energy through the surrounding area. It immediately picked up on the foul demonic imprint that the hound's presence left behind. I couldn't see it so much as feel it, like a long string of spider web. I reached out my right hand until it was level with the metaphysical residue and the signal strengthened. It was definitely here, in these woods, tonight. No way in hell we were going to sneak up on it, not with its sense of smell and excellent hearing. We'd have to lure it out instead.

We traveled for about a mile before I sensed we were close enough for the hound to know we were there. I stopped dead.

Jordan bumped into me and made a startled sound. "What gives?"

"So," I said, turning toward her. "How do you feel about being bait?"

"Not my first choice, but I can handle it. What do you need me to do?"

"Look past my right shoulder. About ten yards off, near that big dead log."

Her brown eyes searched and found what I'd described. She swallowed. "Oh."

"Yeah," I said, lowering my voice to a bare whisper. "He's waiting for us to get closer. If we take him head on, it's not going to go well. I'll head to my right. I want you to stay here and tempt him."

She arched an eyebrow. "Tempt how? Strip to my undies and start singing the 'Oh Wolfy' song from *Swing Shift Cinderella*?"

I rolled my eyes. "Count to twenty and then make a small cut on the inside of your wrist. The blood will work him into a frenzy and he'll come for you—"

"—and then you'll grab him. Right. I hate you and I hate this plan, but for the good of humanity, I'll do it. If you let him eat me, I'm gonna haunt the crap out of you."

I tucked a stray strand of hair behind her ear. "He's not going to lay a paw on you. I promise."

She took a deep breath. "Okay. Get going, pretty boy."

I headed into the woods to my right. I got a few steps before I caught the faint sound of Jordan singing the lyrics to that old Tex Avery cartoon she mentioned. What a dork.

I counted to twenty under my breath during my trek and then stood still. I concentrated on releasing my inner energy until my silver-white wings sprung free from between my shoulder blades. It felt like growing an extra pair of limbs, and yet it satisfied an odd itch that I always encountered in my human body. I missed the days when man knew about us angels and I could freely walk among them in my natural form.

I clicked off my flashlight and launched myself into the air, dodging stray branches and weaving between the trees until I reached the canopy.

Jordan stood a few yards away where I'd left her, and the hellhound lay hunched in attack position. I watched her lift the knife enough to cut herself.

The hound's head lifted from near the ground and its jaws creaked open like a crocodile trying to cool itself on a hot day in the swamp. Its sharp teeth glistened in the faint moonlight, as did its blood-red eyes. Its entire shaggy body shuddered, and it began creeping toward her.

"Come on, you son of a bitch," I murmured, closing my fingers around my weapon. I'd given Jordan my drop knife, which was great as a concealed weapon in close quarters, but the one I used for protection was a combat knife. I'd only started carrying one since the incident with the Spear, and I'd found this one to be the most effective. Hellhounds were tough, but they were still flesh-and-blood. I'd have one clear shot at him to get the job done, or else things would get messy.

The hound closed in until it was less than ten feet from Jordan. She sank into a defensive position with the knife, holding her forearm out so the blood would spill in front of her.

The beast lunged for her. I twisted in the air and dove for it at breakneck speed, slicing through the air like an arrow.

I smashed into the hellhound when it was less than three feet away from Jordan and wrapped both arms around its massive barrel chest. I plunged the knife into its throat and twisted it hard. A strangled roar belted from the demonic creature, and then it sank its teeth right into my left shoulder.

We landed in a struggling heap in the underbrush, kicking up loam and sending dead leaves flying around us. The hound lay on its back beneath me, slashing at my abdomen with its claws and digging its fangs deeper into my flesh. The sharp pain sliced through my upper body. My blood dripped down to mix with his on my hands and arms. The knife's handle started to slide in my grip.

I tore the blade free and reared back to stab him again, but it caught a glancing blow across the side of my face with one of its huge paws. The sheer force of it rolled us over and in seconds, the hound fell upon me.

I shoved my forearm into its wide mouth to protect my throat and cried out as it bit me again, shaking its head to try and rip my arm out of its socket. My knife had fallen in the melee, so I punched the creature in the eye with my free hand, trying to hurt it enough to get loose. It snarled and latched down harder on my arm until blood spilled into my face, partially blinding me.

"Hey, fur-face!"

The hound's ears perked up and its head turned to the right just as Jordan swung a fallen tree branch with all her might. The limb knocked the creature into a tree beside us with a sickening crunch. The beast crumpled onto its side among the tree's roots.

Jordan lunged for the kill with my recovered combat knife. She stabbed it in the chest until her hands were crimson. The hellhound died with a mournful, hair-raising howl and then evaporated into a steaming pile of ash. Jordan stood up on shaky feet and dropped my knife before shuffling over to me.

She knelt and pulled me into a sitting position. The cold air had slowed some of the bleeding, but every single scratch and bite wound throbbed and stung like someone had dumped hydrochloric acid on me.

"What would you do without me?" she asked.

I offered her a weak smile. "I honestly don't know. Now do you understand why I didn't want to take him head on?"

"Definitely. Hold still." She laid her hand on my torn up shoulder. I flinched and she apologized before pouring healing energy into the wound. My skin tingled and then slowly began to close up. I didn't have to let her do this for me. I could have healed myself, but I didn't after I'd seen the fear in her brown eyes.

"Nice touch with the tree branch," I said. "Very Wonder Woman."

She shook her head at me, but the comment made her smile. "Well, I couldn't let him shred you into beef jerky. Wouldn't want Gabriel on my case."

"Yeah, he sure can fuss when he wants to."

Once the shoulder bite had healed, she moved on to my forearm. Chunks of flesh had been torn out. If she hadn't stopped him when she did, I'd have needed a blood transfusion. Or a new arm.

"How do you do this?"

I met her solemn gaze this time. "Do what?"

"I saw your face while you were fighting that thing. You didn't hesitate. You weren't scared. What's that like, being fearless?"

I licked my lips. "Means getting your ass kicked a lot until you get better. And I'm not fearless. I'm just...persistent."

"Is that why you're so determined to get Winters?"

"Damn straight. Someone who could make a monster like that—" I nodded in the direction of the ash heap. "–doesn't deserve to keep breathing. He's going to pay dearly for what he's done."

"Amen." Once my arm was smooth and unblemished once again, Jordan's gaze dropped to my chest. The hounds' claws ripped gigantic holes into my long-sleeved shirt, and beneath them were several gashes. They weren't nearly as deep as the bites, but they still hurt like a bitch. However, I could tell she seemed to be debating with herself on whether she'd feel comfortable groping me. I bit my lip to keep from smiling.

"I can get these ones," I told her. "Thanks."

She brushed my disheveled hair away from my brow, revealing the scrapes the beast left when it hit me in the face. "You sure?"

I caught her hand and she met my eyes again. Her skin was cool to the touch and still wet with blood, and so was mine. The longer my fingers held hers, the warmer they became. We were inches apart, breathing in sync, lost in the quiet world of the forest. Words crawled up my throat and crowded my tongue, words I had no business saying and never would, but they were still there, waiting.

"Yeah," I whispered—an intimate sound in the darkness. "I'm fine."

I stood and helped her up. I squeezed her fingers once, briefly, before letting go. Then we left the forest in search of the real monster.

GREED II

I awoke to the melodic notes of "My Beloved Monster" by Eels at what I considered to be an ungodly hour, if you'll excuse the pun. My arm immediately lashed out towards the nightstand to silence the ringtone that indicated someone sarcastic, defensive, and pretty was calling at seven o'clock in the morning.

My fingers gripped the phone and dragged it across the surface of my mattress until it reached my ear.

"What?" I growled with all the tender sweetness of a lion that had been recently castrated. Without anesthesia. By a pet store sales clerk.

"You know that demon who set that hellhound on those people?"

"Yeah."

"He's here."

I sat up so quickly it made me dizzy. "What did you just say?"

"He's sitting in a booth at the restaurant. And he specifically asked for me."

Jordan's voice resembled piano wire — so tight with anger that it could snap at any given second. Nothing stirred the fire in her veins like a bad guy hanging around innocent people.

I threw off the covers and grabbed the nearest pair of jeans on the floor, hopping into them as I spoke. "Has he said anything about the case yet?"

"No. Just asked for coffee."

"Stay on him. I'll be there in a blink. If he even lifts a finger, douse his ass with holy water and get the hell out of there."

She adopted an offended tone. "I'm not going to leave these people here as sitting ducks."

I gritted my teeth, struggling into a t-shirt. "Damn it, Jordan, this is your life we're talking about—"

"—and it's *their* lives I'm talking about, so can it and get your ass over here pronto, *burro terco*."

Translation: stubborn jackass. Nice. Jordan got very sarcastic when she was stressed or angry. So did I. "Hey, pot? Kettle says you're looking a little black around the edges."

"You're hilarious. Get a move on, archangel."

She hung up. I stuffed the phone into my pocket along with my keys, wallet, and other essentials: a couple vials of holy water, an angel feather, and my Green Beret knife. Technically, it would be safer to have a gun, but I had always been faster with a blade. The clunky weight of a firearm never quite felt natural to me.

Long ago, emergencies meant sprouting my wings and flying to a destination. Now, I lived in the middle of the crowded, heavily monitored streets of Albany. No way in hell I could fly and not be seen by dozens of people, with cell phones no less.

I shut my apartment door, locked it, and stood still in the empty hallway. I calculated the distance between the restaurant and my place before utilizing my enhanced agility. Luckily, the streets weren't crowded since it was so early, allowing me more cover to run just under the speed to break the sound barrier. I arrived at the Sweet Spot in three minutes flat.

To my relief, I didn't spot any screaming people running out into the street or bloodstains on the windows. In fact, the restaurant's atmosphere seemed perfectly normal.

Only Jordan and I could have sensed the pulsating demonic power emanating from Jean Winters.

Beth greeted me as I walked in and I told her I was meeting a gentleman here for breakfast. She led me over to the man himself. On my way to the seat, I'd counted how many people were here: twelve customers and ten employees, including Jordan. If things went sideways, I had plenty of lives riding on it. Then again, I suspected that was Winters' entire point.

Winters had slicked back dark brown hair, olive skin, and unnervingly large hands. Gold rings glinted on every finger. Each one had a symbol engraved in demonspeak for his sin of choice: greed. He wore an impeccable dark blue suit with a yellow-and-white striped tie.

His brown eyes held a calculating glint as they flicked up from the coffee mug to meet my gaze. "Ah. Michael. How nice of you to join me."

"Wouldn't miss it for the world," I said, sliding into the seat across from him. Beth let me know Jordan would be by in a moment and then returned to her place at the front.

I went for the casual approach. "You seem to be keeping well."

Winters smiled. "Business has been booming. I've been a fortunate man these last few years, at least since the last time we crossed paths."

"Glad to hear it." I settled one hand on my thigh, ready to pull out the knife at any given second. The other I occupied with my silverware to perpetuate the illusion that I was here to eat.

I didn't see a suspicious bulge beneath his suit jacket. If he was carrying, it wasn't a gun. Demons often relied on their superhuman strength to get results. He could try to tear my head off and punt it out the window if he wanted to, but it would be ill-advised. Judging by the way he stared me down, he knew I was armed.

Footsteps. Jordan appeared to my right. She had perfected the art of the cute, bubbly waitress years prior. Seeing her smile so sweetly still freaked me out a bit.

"How are you boys doing?"

"Magnificently," Winters replied, warming his voice. "The coffee is as delicious as you said, my dear."

"Would you like to order breakfast yet?"

"Not quite. I'm still perusing the menu." He made a show of letting his eyes drag down her body from head to toe. The typical uniform at the Sweet Spot was a white dress shirt, black skirt, a smock, and flat shoes. The dress code was lenient on the type of skirt. Jordan usually went between a pencil skirt that hit her at the knees and a flowing one that drew attention to her hips on days where she wanted a really good tip. Today, she'd chosen the latter. The heat in Winters' eyes could have made the coffee boil in its mug. The look was so unabashedly scummy that I half-expected to see a trail of slime left behind where his gaze touched her. Anger rushed through me in a scalding wave.

"Not a problem," Jordan said, unfazed by his leering. "I'll be back to check on you in a moment."

Before she left, Jordan's hand brushed my shoulder. I glanced down and realized I'd gripped the spoon so hard that I bent it in half. I quickly fixed it and then returned my gaze to the demon in front of me.

"Now that we've exchanged pleasantries, do you mind telling me what you want?"

He lifted his eyebrows. "Want, dear boy?"

"You didn't come all the way down here for the coffee," I said, allowing some of the torrid wrath inside me to seep through my voice. "It's good, but not that damn good. How did you find out I was investigating the hellhound killings?"

"A man in my position only gets there by having ears and eyes everywhere. You've made quite a splash in the brief time that you've been in this city. It hasn't gone unnoticed by my kind."

"If you know that, then you know I've been working a lot of cases lately. What made you decide to show your face?"

His faux pleasant demeanor changed into stark fury. His thick brows angled downward, his thin lips peeled back from his teeth, and wrinkles bunched on his forehead. "I spent quite a lot of time training that hound to obey me. Boagreus was loyal, efficient, and ruthless. *Lex talionis.*"

That last phrase was Latin for "eye for an eye." He wanted to kill Jordan because she'd killed his hound. I balled my hands into fists hard enough to leave marks in my palm. "Did you just compare Jordan Amador, the Seer who saved my life, *to your dog?*"

Winters cocked his head to the side. "What? You mean she isn't your pet?"

"Watch your mouth," I whispered.

He continued as if I hadn't said anything. "She must be. Look at her. Full of life and vitality. Blindly loyal to her master. Tell me...does she come when you call?"

In the blink of an eye, I had my knife out with its tip pressed against the inside of his right knee. "Go ahead. Say one more thing about her. You'll be dragging bloody stumps out the front door. Someone will have to come back to get what's left of your tongue out of the garbage disposal."

Winters laughed. "Colorful. I didn't know she meant that much to you."

The humor evaporated as quickly as it had come. "We need to come to an understanding. I will not hesitate to protect my interests just as I know you will not hesitate to protect that which is most precious to you. You need to make a choice, archangel. Justice or her safety. You cannot have both. I am not the discreet man that you knew in Atlanta. I will find where she is most vulnerable. I will take her from you, and I will make you watch. This is your only warning to stay out of my affairs."

"You think this is the first time scum like you threatened someone I care about?" I snarled. "Get in line, asshole. If you want to play this game, then understand that it won't be moving chess pieces on a board. If you come for her, I'm going to peel your skin off and feed it to you. The last thing you will ever taste will be your own blood before I send you crawling back to Hell where you belong."

I leaned forward, digging the blade into his knee until I heard the fabric of his pants rip. "Do you understand me, demon?"

He watched me for a while, as if gauging the weight behind my words. "Very well. Then you have made your choice."

Jordan returned with a pot of coffee. "Let me freshen that up for you."

She refilled his mug. Winters continued staring at me as he drank it. Then his brown eyes went as wide as plates and he spit out a mouthful onto the table. He made a strangled sound of pain and vapor burst from the inside of his mouth. I caught a glimpse of blisters on his tongue as if he'd gotten second degree burns.

"Oh, dear," Jordan said with false concern. "Too hot for you, sir?"

He aimed a death glare at her before stumbling to his feet and storming out of the restaurant. I glanced at her in surprise as she watched him stomp down the street.

"What'd you do?"

She tapped her nails against the coffee pot, her smile utterly satisfied. "Slipped some holy water into his coffee."

I shook my head. "That was reckless."

"Had to get him out of here somehow."

The amusement drained out of her face, leaving it solemn. "What did he want?"

I slipped my knife back into its hiding place and sighed. "To declare war."

"On the city?"

"On you."

She frowned. "Oh, come on. Really?"

"Really."

She sighed. "This is what I get for killing a dog, I guess."

"You should probably be a little more worried."

"Don't see why."

I stared at her. A small smile touched her lips. "It's not like my babysitter is going to let the boogeyman get me."

"Things might get nasty."

"Been there, done that." She brought over a new mug and poured me some coffee. "On the house. You look like you could use some caffeine."

She touched my shoulder once more, but this time I felt the difference. She squeezed it with her fingers for the briefest of seconds, rubbing her thumb along my shirt collar. I knew what that meant. *I trust you. I've got your back. We're going to be alright.*

Ass-deep in murderous creatures and she still had faith in me. Small wonders.

"Thanks," I said. Then I drank my coffee and prepared for war.

GREED III

I had managed to avoid any extensive time in the retail world until I took this job as Jordan's bodyguard. There was a reason for that. Working for a pathetic salary and dealing with broke musicians, immature teenagers with dirty hands, and snotty producers shopping for the most expensive instruments they could find wore me down day in and day out. I could have opted for a career in anything after I got my soul and memories back, but retail left open a window. I could get time off at the drop of a hat in case of emergencies, and it didn't require excessive amounts of devotion so I could concentrate on other things.

My eyelids nearly closed as I stood at the front door to my apartment, fumbling for my keys. Eight hour shift today. I wanted nothing more than to sleep until the wee hours of the morning. A needling sensation poked my grey matter as I opened the door and locked it behind me. I was supposed to be remembering something. No idea what, though.

The only other thing I could think of was that we still hadn't seen any action from Jean Winters after his threat at the Sweet Spot last week. The angels in the local P.D. had been working around the clock to prove his involvement with the recent hellhound murders, but they'd come up empty so far. Hard to prove anything without the creature's body. The only evidence linking him was his office's client list. We needed something better to go on or Winters would walk, and Jordan's life remained in constant danger until then.

I kicked off my shoes in the den and shuffled into the kitchen. I drained the entire carton of orange juice in the fridge and then headed towards the closed bedroom door. Odd. I didn't remember closing it before I left this morning.

I opened the door and reached to turn on the light.

Six silenced gun shots went off.

Pain. So…much…*pain*.

I collapsed to the floor with my shoulders, arms, and chest lit aflame in agony. Every breath came in choked gasps. At least one shot had hit one of my lungs. Blood poured out of every wound and soaked into my work shirt, my carpet, my slacks. *Stupid, stupid, stupid, Michael.*

I rolled onto my side as the floorboards in my room creaked, indicating movement. A brunette woman with a pageboy haircut emerged. She wore a black leather jacket and leggings over combat boots. Her pale face would have been pretty if not for the psychotic smile on her red lips.

"Welcome home, honey," the woman purred, kneeling in front of me. "How was your day?"

I glared at her, struggling to stay conscious as the pain ate its way from my torso up through my neck and into my brain. She had the drop on me, but didn't go for a killing shot. Why?

"What…do you…want?" I rasped.

She smoothed her gloved fingers through my hair almost lovingly. "To make you suffer, sweetheart. Slowly. After all, that's what I was hired to do."

I tried to say something else, but she laid a finger on my lips. "Rest. We'll talk when you wake up."

No, my brain screamed. *Don't you dare pass out. Stay conscious. Stay conscious, damn it!*

Too little too late. I blacked out seconds later, still yelling at myself not to.

I woke up chained to the support pillar in my kitchen. The counter and sink were connected in an upside down L-shape, leaving the corner of the breakfast bar to dig into the back of my shoulder blades. The bullets still burned everything inside me that they touched like hot glowing coals. I had a handkerchief tied tightly around my head to gag me. The dried blood on my shirt meant I'd been out for a while.

The woman wasn't a demon. I'd blessed the apartment myself. At the very least, she was a professional.

The small grunts of pain escaping me alerted my captor that I was awake. She sat cross-legged on the couch, polishing the barrel of her gun. Her brown eyes lit up and the sick smile returned. I noticed a beauty mark on her right cheek. Still, her face didn't ring a bell. Not a local hit-woman, it seemed. I knew them from the police files.

"Oh, good," she said with a honeyed voice, standing up and walking towards me. "You're up. How are you feeling?"

I gave her nothing but an infuriated stare. She pouted, guiding her gaze down at my blood-soaked torso. "You must be in terrible pain. Let's have a look-see."

She reached to the small of her back and whipped out a butterfly knife, flipping it open with expert movements. She slashed my shirt from collar to hem, spreading the cloth apart. Six bullets were embedded in my upper body. I still couldn't breathe well, but my body had healed some of the damage to my lungs. Otherwise, I'd have drowned in my own blood while I was passed out.

"Doesn't look good, boss," the hit-woman said, clucking her tongue. "Let's see if we can fix that."

She jammed the knife into the wound in my right pectoral. I couldn't help it. I screamed through the gag as the

~ 94 ~

pain intensified so hard that my arms started shaking. She twisted it until the slug popped free with a wet '*schlock*' and hit the carpet. Fresh blood gurgled out of the gaping hole left behind.

"Much better." She stroked the side of my face. "How do you feel now?"

Again, I kept silent. "I bet you have some questions for me, huh? That's fine. I know you're not stupid enough to scream for help because I'll slit your neighbors' throats if they come over."

She untied the handkerchief. I swallowed a couple times before speaking. "If you're going to kill me, just do it. I don't have time for the games."

"But the games are what I like, Michael, dear. That's why I agreed to this job. I've never gotten a contract on an archangel before, just some of the lowly regular ones. I want to see what makes you so tough. You can take a lot of punishment, can't you?"

"You have no idea."

She flattened her hands against the beam on either side of my head, leaning her lithe form up against me. "I bet you can. I've never met a man I couldn't kill. Winters told me you'd be good sport. I'm praying that's the case."

"You're human. There are a thousand other things you could be doing, and yet you chose this life. Why?"

She shrugged. "I like the challenge. I like knowing that at any second, I could die, and the thrill that comes when I don't."

The hit-woman trailed her fingertips down the center of my chest until she cupped my groin. "I'm sure you do too, handsome."

"You have no idea who you're dealing with, lady," I whispered. "I will give you exactly one chance to leave here alive. Be smart. Take it."

"My name's not 'lady.' It's Liz. And I appreciate the offer, but no deal. The reward I was promised is too sweet to give up."

I tensed as she continued rubbing me below the belt. "What reward?"

She finally removed the roving hand, to my relief. "Why, Michael. So forward. I'd never do something so wicked, not with a taken man."

Ice water flooded through my veins. "Taken?"

"Don't sound so surprised. I know all about your little chippie. She's cute, but I'm surprised you went for someone so average. I mean, she's not even a C-cup—"

I threw myself at her on impulse, straining my shoulders and sending shock waves of pain down my front in the process. "If you laid a hand on her, I'll—"

Liz made a scoffing sound in the back of her throat. "Why on earth would I kill her without you there to watch? Why do you think I came to your place?"

It dawned on me then what I'd forgotten. I told Jordan to come over to discuss our game plan for taking down Winters. The clock on the wall read five minutes to nine. *God, no.*

She smiled. "You've got people in the police and people in the NSA. So do we. It wasn't difficult to get a wiretap. Child's play, really."

Five minutes. Jordan would die for my mistake in five minutes if I didn't stop it. I needed a plan. The chains wouldn't break, but the way she bound me left my hands out of sight. My best bet was to slip an arm free and rip her damn throat out. *Keep her distracted. Keep her talking. Buy as much time as you can.*

"If you kill us, it's all going to point back to Winters," I said, slowly starting to wiggle my wrist back and forth to test the bonds. The blood that dripped down my arms from earlier hadn't dried completely yet. It could help lubricate the chains. I dug my nails into my arm until it tore the skin and fresh blood leaked out.

"He knows. That's why he's going to fake his own death and move to a new body. That money isn't going anywhere in the meantime."

The predatory glint in her eyes flickered on again. "Now then, where were we? Right."

She stabbed me in the gut, fishing for the second bullet, and shoved her hand over my mouth to muffle my scream. Once the slug slid out, she gave me a kiss and stroked my cheek. "Shh, it's over. Wasn't so bad, right?"

A buzzing sound drew our attention to the kitchen countertop where my phone lay. "My Beloved Monster" by Eels broke the sudden silence. *No.*

Liz scooped up the phone and held her blade at my Adam's apple. "Let's not be rude. If you warn her not to come, I'll kill her slowly. Be a good boy and say hi to your girlfriend."

She answered the call and held it up to my ear. I steadied my breath and spoke. "Hello?"

"Hey, I'm running a little late," Jordan said, sounding winded as if she'd been chasing after the bus. "Should be there in five."

"Fine," I said, staring at Liz. "See you when you get here. I love you."

Liz hung up. "Aw. So affectionate. I can see why she fell for you."

"Guess I'm just a sentimental guy." Couple inches of slack at my right wrist. Almost there.

"We've got a little more time to kill with your baby running late. Shall we go for the next bullet?"

"If you like a challenge so much, why not untie me? Come at me honestly."

She batted her eyelashes. "I'm a murderer, not an idiot. Even with those wounds, you're still too fast and too strong. I don't want a minute man. Besides, you're ridiculously gorgeous when you're all tied up and bloody. I might have to take a picture and use it as my phone background."

I couldn't reply because she jabbed the knife into me a third time, removing the slug in my upper chest. It hurt more than the others as the bullet had sunk deep into the tissue. My eyes watered and the world swam in my vision. My hands and wrists fell slack for a moment from the sheer intensity of the pain.

"Oh, don't tell me that took the fight out of you," Liz said, lifting my chin with her hand. "Three left, big boy. This is all the fun I get tonight. Your girlfriend won't get to see the show."

"W-What?" I managed through convulsive, gulping breaths.

"Torturing you is my payment. Winters knows there isn't a way to kill an angel permanently yet. After you return to earth with a new body, you might be able to hunt him down if you put your mind to it. That's why he wants me to just shoot your girlfriend in cold blood. He wants you to watch her die, knowing that you failed her. No long, dramatic death scene. Just a click and a boom and she's gone. It hurts more when we die without a word, without knowing why. You know that. You've seen it a thousand times."

She pushed the hair out of my eyes. The teasing finally abated. I saw the monster inside her up close and personal now. "So tell me, Michael. Are you a weak man? Will you beg me to spare your lady love? Will you bargain with me for her life?"

Something rattled around in my ribs. It bubbled up my aching chest cavity before spilling out from between my lips. Laughter.

Surprise skittered across her face. I stopped long enough to draw breath to talk. "The only thing crazier than you, Elizabeth, is the idea that I'd insult Jordan's honor by begging for mercy. I want to make one thing perfectly clear. If you do manage to kill her, there is no crevasse that you can hide in where I will not find you. I am not just some handsome bodyguard. I am the archangel Michael. I am the Prince of Heaven's Army. I am the Commander. I will swallow you whole and spit out your bones like the thousands of others foolish enough to cross me. Do your worst, little girl. See what happens."

The hit-woman said nothing, instead staring at me as if I'd grown a second head, and it was currently trying to eat the first one. I let what was left of my spiritual energy leak out of me and consume her entire form. She wouldn't know it, but she'd feel a cold air creeping into her lungs like poisonous gas. I got the sense she'd done this dozens of times before, torturing victims who fell for her act. Not me. For the first time, she seemed to grasp the gravity of what she'd gotten herself into.

The doorbell rang.

The now-panicked Liz picked up the Beretta and emptied the clip at the front door.

~ 99 ~

Seconds later, I heard the unmistakable thud of something hitting the ground.

No.

Please, God, no.

Liz's breathing came high and thready when she walked towards the entrance, reloading the gun as she went. I couldn't move. This wasn't happening. I couldn't have failed her again. I couldn't have lost her again.

The hit-woman opened the door. No dead body on the floor. *Thank God.*

I heard an unearthly roar and then Jordan charged Liz from where she'd been hiding beside the door. She tackled her to the floor and stabbed her through the wrist with a small switchblade. The hit-woman shrieked and let go of the gun, allowing Jordan precious seconds to bat it across the room. She landed a couple hard punches to the assassin's nose, bloodying it, before the other woman got the upper hand.

She grabbed a handful of Jordan's ponytail and slammed her head into the edge of the coffee table. Jordan cried out, but didn't let go of the knife. She withdrew it and held it against the assassin's throat, shouting, "Move again and I'll kill you, *puta!*"

Liz panted madly, but stayed put. Jordan glanced up at me. "You okay?"

"Alive," I said through a grimace. "Not okay."

"Good enough." She returned her gaze to the woman pinned beneath her and glared.

"The police are on their way. And not the nice, human police. Angels. Get any ideas about trying to kill me again and you won't even get to deal with them."

"I've been in jail before," Liz said, attempting to recapture her former arrogance. "I'll get over it."

Jordan leaned down a few inches, lowering her voice. "Really? How'd you like to return without your tongue?"

Liz's eyes went wide, as did mine. "You wouldn't dare."

"You shot my best friend. Multiple times. *Lex talionis*."

"You can't kill me. You're not a policewoman. You're just a girl."

"No. I'm a Seer. You and the rest of your friends had better learn the difference between a sheep and a wolf in sheep's clothing. Until then…"

She lifted her fist and punched Liz hard in the temple. The assassin went out like a light.

"*Vaya con dios*, bitch."

Jordan stood and rolled the unconscious Liz onto her stomach, tying her up with the drawstring to my robe that she found dangling off the couch. She kicked the door shut and came over to me, examining the chains. She gave a start when she realized I already had one arm free.

"You let me do that on my own, even though you could have stopped her."

I nodded. She smiled. "You're so sweet it hurts sometimes."

A shaky laugh escaped me as she helped slide the chains off. I wobbled and swayed until she helped me sit on the couch. The soft cushions welcomed my sore back, but the pain in my chest was the main issue. The wounds throbbed at a constant rate, and the ones Liz had reopened gushed blood every few seconds.

"How'd you know I was in trouble?" I asked.

She gave me a 'D'uh' look. "'I love you?' Seriously, this is not a Nicholas Sparks novel. No way in hell you'd say that to me unless you were about to die."

"Glad you caught that."

"Glad you were smart enough to think of it." With that, Jordan vanished into my bathroom and returned with rubbing alcohol, towels, and my First Aid kit. She reached for my chest, but I caught her hand in mine. She met my eyes.

"Thank you."

She shook her head. "Don't. If I'd have gotten here sooner—"

"Shut up," I whispered hoarsely, cupping the right side of her cheek. "Can't you just say 'you're welcome' like a normal person?"

Slowly, she relaxed beneath my fingers. She touched the back of my hand. "You're welcome, Michael."

I bumped her forehead with mine, not giving a damn about whatever lines it might have blurred in our relationship. She was alive and she had saved my ass again. At this point, I wasn't sure who was protecting whom, but then again, I didn't care.

And maybe that was the point all along.

SLOTH

I couldn't tell if my current predicament was a sin or not. Probably. Maybe. Things were supposed to be clear cut when you're an archangel, but the more time I spent on earth as a man, the more I realized there were a lot of grey areas.

I had to be at work in half an hour. Which meant taking a shower, getting dressed, scarfing down breakfast, and taking the bus downtown. It would be the responsible thing to do instead of taking the day off. I knew that much, at least. It was only a seven-hour shift and I'd be home to catch up on some rest.

My problem was that I had just woken up on the couch in my apartment with my best friend draped over me like a living blanket.

Jordan slept like the dead. Nothing short of a train crashing with a plane on top of a nuclear testing site could wake her up in the morning. Thus, if I got up to go to work, she wouldn't even feel it. So that wasn't the issue here. The issue was that I was very comfortable in this spot on the couch, more comfortable than I should have been with a girl who was just my friend. Or, rather, the only Seer on Earth at the moment who needed my protection.

I could tell what had happened, too — sometime during the night, we were reclining side-by-side on the couch and I fell asleep first, meaning I had shifted to lie with my head on the arm. Jordan clearly forgot to go home and slumped over. In my sleep, I'd moved to accommodate her body so she ended up tucked into my side during the night. Right now, that meant the top of her head brushed my chin, one hand lying on my chest, the other somewhere under the side of her body, and one of her legs had curled around my right knee to get more comfy as she slept. Plus, we were both fully clothed, so it probably wasn't a sin.

Probably.

Then again, my arm had wound around her waist and my hand rested on the small of her back, perilously close to what Sterling Archer would call the Danger Zone. My self-control was unmatched, but not endless. No matter what I decided, my hand needed to move. Period.

Minutes dripped off the clock on my wall. I continued staring at it, wondering what to do. Then out of nowhere, I heard a soft, sleepy voice.

"Don't you have to go to work?"

I closed my eyes for a second, trying not to smile. "Yeah."

Jordan sighed, a burst of hot air against my neck, and didn't move an inch. "So go to work."

"I can't."

"Why?"

"I have a cold."

"No, you don't."

"When did you go to med school?"

She made a snorting sound similar to a laugh. "Fine. But you're not moving in with me after you get fired."

"I'm basically living with you anyway."

"Mm."

"Jordan?"

"Yeah?"

"Go back to sleep."

"Mmkay."

Yeah. Definitely a sin.

SLOTH II

"Jordan!"

"What?"

"I can't write!"

Silence. I lay spread eagle on my bed with my acoustic guitar across my stomach and my head hanging off one end of the mattress. The tone in my voice was more than pathetic. Whiny. Childish. Nothing like the Commander who could make demons crap their pants from forty paces away. If Father could see me now.

"What the hell do you want me to do about it?" Jordan called back from the den. My bedroom door was open, but I couldn't quite see her. The doorway was across from the kitchen instead of the den, after all.

"Inspire me or something."

"When did I become your Muse?"

I thought about it. She had a point. "You're human. What do regular human musicians do when they can't write songs?"

Movement. The leather cushion squeaked as Jordan's lithe body vacated it. I listened to the sound of her bare feet padding across the carpet. She appeared a moment later with a can of Pepsi in one hand and an expression somewhere between annoyance and amusement. My apartment was always a bit warm, due to the faulty air conditioning system, so her hair was piled up in a messy bun and she had on a pair of shorts underneath her oversized white t-shirt. My upside-down position allowed me just the barest glimpse of her bellybutton. She had an innie, as they called it. Interesting.

"Get drunk. Shag bimbos. Smoke weed and listen to Pink Floyd. And that's just off the top of my head." She sipped her soda while I frowned at her.

"Pretty sure everything you just listed is a sin."

She offered me a sly look. "Musicians tend to be awful good at sinning, I hear."

I sighed and closed my eyes. "Are you always this useless?"

"Only to you." I heard the soda can click as she set it on the nightstand. The bed tipped to one side. She'd climbed on. The rasp of papers moving indicated that she'd found some of the lyrics I had tried in vain to work on.

"Well, here's your first problem," she said. "Your subject matter is all over the place."

I lurched upright and then propped the guitar up against my pillow. "Pardon?"

"I can't tell if this song is about a girl or about music."

"Why can't it be both?"

"It can if you clean up your metaphors. Your lyrics lack focus. That's why you can't write anything, Aerosmith."

I scowled and snatched the page from her. "And just what do you know about good lyrics? I missed you at the Grammy Awards last year."

"Ha-ha," she said, rolling her eyes. "I happen to have excellent taste in music, I'll have you know."

"I seem to recall hearing Antonio Banderas' 'Cancion del Mariachi' in your music library, so I think that might be a slight hyperbole."

She blanched, as much as a black girl can. "When did you...?"

I offered her my most devilish grin. "I might have been awake that day you were singing in the kitchen."

She buried her face in her hands. "This is what I get for giving you a key."

I chuckled. "Relax. It was by far the most adorable, awkward thing I've ever seen."

She flopped onto her stomach, her voice muffled. "I hate you."

I picked my guitar back up and adjusted the tuning pegs. "Your hatred fills me with inspiration. Thank you, Jordan."

I strummed a few notes and then started singing the lyrics to "She Hates Me" by Puddle of Mudd until Jordan sat up and whacked me with a pillow. The abject humiliation on her face sent me into a bout of laughter and she hit me again. I flipped the guitar and used it as a shield. Eventually, she gave up and collapsed next to me sideways on the bed. We lay there in a comfortable silence, staring at the poster of Jimmy Hendrix on my far wall.

"You're right, though," I said. "It's not clear. Not sure why. It usually comes to me so easily when I write."

"Something must be blocking you. Writers get it all the time. Might be stress. Might be pure laziness too."

I shot her a glare. "Hey, when's the last time you sang for your supper?"

"If I had to rely on my singing skills to pay rent, I'd be homeless and dead in a week. Couldn't carry a tune if it was super-glued to my hand."

"Want some lessons?"

"No thanks. The starving artist quota is already filled in this relationship."

"Point taken." I slid the guitar off my belly again and groaned. "Ugh. Still can't think of anything to write about."

Jordan rolled over and propped her arms on my chest so she could look down at me. "Then why don't you edit some old songs until you get in the mood?"

"Don't feel like it."

"You are such a big baby."

"Do you have any functions other than nagging?"

"Hey, you asked for help."

"I asked for inspiration."

"And I told you what normal musicians do for inspiration."

I met her gaze with utter deadpan. "Well, I guess we'll just have to have sex then, won't we?"

She didn't even bat an eyelash—merely gazing back at me with a cool look in her dark brown eyes. "Guess so."

A staring contest ensued. Then my phone rang. I fished it out of my pocket and answered it, cursing myself for being the first to look away.

"Yeah?"

"Michael," my brother Gabriel said without his usual polite candor. "Are you busy?"

I glanced back up at Jordan with my sleaziest grin. "No, but I'm getting there."

She rolled her eyes again and pushed off my chest to sit cross-legged next to me. I heaved upright and pushed a wayward cloud of hair out of my eyes.

"What is it?"

"I am in need of your assistance. Do you remember Adira Mahmood?"

I paused. "About five foot nothing, pretty eyes, nose ring?"

"Yes. She and I had been working on tracking a particularly nasty pack of demons who were involved with a local gang of drug traffickers. She was supposed to meet me for dinner and she has not shown. Her phone goes straight to voicemail. I am worried she's been compromised. Could you look into it?"

His voice was level, but I caught the edge of apprehension beneath it. "Of course. Text me all of her information and I'll get right on it."

"Thank you, brother. I will meet you as soon as I can. At the moment, I am heading to her apartment to check for signs of foul play."

"Where does she work?"

"She is a bank teller at the Wells Fargo on Winner's Circle. Be careful."

"Ditto. I'll call you soon." I hung up.

Jordan was chewing her bottom lip as she watched me climb off the bed with a certain briskness. "Trouble?"

"Yeah. Got a local angel who's MIA. Better check up on her."

"Don't suppose you could use some backup?"

"Gabriel's covering the other angle," I said, shrugging out of my ratty tank top. "Should be fine. Plus, Adira's no slump. Even if she's in trouble, odds are she won't be in bad shape."

I started to unzip my jeans and then stopped when I realized what I was doing. I turned around to see Jordan watching me with a far-too-casual expression. "Were you going to just let me get half naked in front of you?"

She shrugged. "Didn't want to break your concentration."

I rolled my eyes. "How courteous of you. Out."

"You're so modest for a musician."

"*Out.*"

She slid off the bed and headed towards the door, but lingered in the archway. "I wouldn't mind a bit more experience in the field, y'know. If it's not going to cramp your style."

I couldn't suppress a concerned look from creeping across my features. "You've gotten in enough trouble this month alone. I wouldn't be doing a good job as your bodyguard if I let you come with me."

"Yeah, but what if the bad guys attack while you're gone? I'll be all alone. Woe is me." The last sentence was accompanied by a hand pressed to her forehead in a dramatic yet sardonic gesture.

It didn't take a genius to figure out that she was stir-crazy. It had been over a week since we helped a ghost with unfinished business cross over. I weighed my options. On the one hand, it was a frightfully bad idea to put Jordan in the line of fire when she was the only Seer on earth right now. On the other hand, I could use an extra pair of eyes, especially since it looked to be a missing person's case. Jordan's work as a Seer was essentially like a supernatural private investigator. The recent ruckus with Jean Winters had proven she could handle herself.

"Alright," I conceded. "But only if you let me lead. None of your Lone Ranger heroic stuff."

She held up a hand. "Cross my heart and hope to—"

"Finish that sentence and you're benched."

"Yes, sir."

"Thank you. Now quit staring at my chest and close the door."

She muttered something that sounded like "prude" and shut the door behind her.

After we both got dressed and geared up, I called the Wells Fargo to confirm what time Adira had gotten off work. Her shift ended at six o'clock. It was half past eight by now. Jordan and I took a cab there and began snooping around as inconspicuously as possible near the rear of the building. We found no signs of a struggle, no tire treads like someone had peeled out in a hurry, and no one in the area reported seeing a woman who had been dragged away by bad guys. We did, however, find out she made a stop after getting off work at a local hair salon for a quick style and set, based on the last charge to her credit card.

I was reaching for the door when Jordan touched my shoulder with a cautious look. "Are you sure you don't want me to go in here alone?"

Confused, I glanced between her and the gaggle of women inside. "Why?"

"You're relatively new at this whole human thing. Hair salons are notorious for being troublesome for the male species."

I arched an eyebrow. "I can juggle steamboats. I'm pretty sure I can handle it."

She held up her arms in surrender. "Okay."

I opened the door and she trailed in behind me. The salon was on the small side and could only seat about twelve women. There were four occupants in the chairs and five stylists. The black girl at the front counter was around Jordan's age and gave me a less-than-subtle suspicious look as I walked towards her.

"Hi," I said with my most winning smile. "I was wondering if you could help me real quick."

"You a cop?"

"Ah, no."

She tilted her head enough to see Jordan around my shoulder and then her expression relaxed somewhat. "What can I do for you, honey?"

"My friend accidentally left her cell phone at work and I was hoping to catch up with her before she left town. Her name's Adira. Did she come by here?"

"Yeah, she was in about an hour ago."

"I see. Did she say where she was heading next?"

"Not to me." She angled her head towards the women behind her. "Jackie! Could you c'mere for a second? Brad Pitt here has a question for you."

Jordan made a snorting sound like she was hiding a laugh. One of the stylists—a heavyset woman in her early thirties—came forward with a Cheshire cat grin when she saw me.

"To what do I owe the pleasure?" she asked.

"Adira Mahmood. She's a friend of mine and—"

"Honey, I'm sure *everyone's* a friend of yours."

Again, Jordan made a noise and I ignored her. "—I just need to know if she told you where she was going after she left here."

"You're not a cop, are you?"

I ground my back teeth. "No."

The check in girl nudged the stylist with her elbow. "That's what I said. He sounds like a cop. What'd Adira do?"

"She didn't do anything—"

"Well, she comes here a few times a month and we've never seen you before. You her boyfriend?"

"No, I—"

"Are you trying to get her deported?"

"Of course not—"

"Are you from the credit card company? Are you a lawyer? Nobody comes up in here looking as fine as you do and they're not up to something. So what are you really after?"

Finally, Jordan came forward. "Ladies. A word, please?"

She walked down the aisle between the chairs and they followed. I waited by the counter with my arms crossed, trying to eavesdrop but the conversations from the women in the chairs still getting their hair done filtered it out. Also, the girls in the chairs were having a rather animated discussion about what they wouldn't mind doing to me, so I eventually gave up and went outside.

Jordan returned after a couple of minutes. She wore a patient expression that meant she was trying not to laugh at my expense. "They said Adira caught a cab heading east to the restaurant and that they saw someone following her."

"Did you get a description?"

"Male, early forties, cheap black pinstriped suit, no tie, brown hair, brown eyes. Got into a navy SUV with a Missouri license plate."

"How'd you convince them I wasn't a cop?"

"I didn't."

I frowned. "So why'd they help you? They seemed deeply distrusting of the police."

She smiled and batted her eyelashes. "That's why I gave 'em your phone number. Sweetened the deal."

My jaw dropped and she started down the sidewalk. "You didn't. Jordan. Come on!"

"What? It's perfectly harmless."

"Yeah, unless one of them texts a naughty photo and I have to explain it to my boss," I grumbled as I caught up to her.

She stood near the curb, her nose wrinkled in contemplation as she stared at the bustling street and cluttered traffic. "You said Adira's no slump, right?"

"Right."

"So the only way they'd be able to nab her is if they were in large numbers or through some sort of misdirection."

I nodded, latching onto her theory. "Yeah. There are too many people around this time of night to try for a mob and a big bloody fight. They'd want to keep it quiet and drag her somewhere secluded."

"Can you call your friends in the police department to ask if there were any accidents reported in the area around the time when Adira would've been here?"

"It might take a bit to get that information, but I can try."

I made a couple calls and discovered that there was indeed a car accident not far from here involving a cab driver and a navy SUV. The entire rear of the cab was ruined, and they had to dispatch an ambulance because the cabbie got hurt. The driver supposedly went to apologize to Adira after the EMTs looked her over, but no one recalls seeing either of them after she got out of the ambulance. My instincts told me he made off with her. It wouldn't have been easy, but it was doable.

I hung up the phone once I'd gotten all the information I needed. "The navy SUV is registered to Thomas Wingate. He doesn't have a credit history or any financial statements past this year, so it's definitely a fake ID. Sounds like a demon to me."

Jordan placed her hands on her hips, her legs in a wide stance, dark eyes glittering. Her posture always seemed to change when we had a bad guy to stop. "So what's our next move? How do we find them?"

"Smart demons know not to be hauling an unconscious woman around in broad daylight. Odds are they're holed up somewhere close by with some of his friends. The nearest demon nest to this side of town would be the Lucky Club." I pointed east of us and then beckoned her to follow me across the street.

"A nightclub?" Jordan asked with no small amount of incredulity. "That's cliché even for demons."

I shrugged. "It's loud, crowded, and hard to get into. Clichés are often based on real life, after all."

"If it's a demon's nest, how on earth are a Seer and an archangel going to get in?"

"The fact that you're a Seer is why they'd let you in. I'll just have to suppress my energy until I seem human. Not many demons have seen me in this particular body. We might get lucky. If not, we'll call for back up and storm the place."

I dialed Gabriel and gave him a quick update as we jogged the four blocks to the club. It was a hole-in-the-wall kind of place, practically dripping with the promise of a sticky dance floor, smoke-clogged air, and bad electronic music. He told me he was on his way and I hung up as we turned the last corner to the front. Green neon lights beamed down at us as we walked along the sidewalk to the Lucky Club, which completed the stereotype by having a four-leaf clover surrounding the name.

The line was reasonable as far as clubs go because it was so hard to get in. Humans were only allowed in if they were prey. Anyone who could take care of themselves would be turned away, so I'd have to play a role if I wanted to pass. I'd buried my spiritual energy as deep as I could about a block away so that none of them would sense me coming. I hadn't taught Jordan how to do it quite yet, but we were getting there.

"What's the plan?" Jordan murmured as she undid her ponytail and shook out her hair.

"I'll lead. They'll have put her in one of the private rooms. We'll have a look around and see if we can find her without causing too much of a fuss."

She fished her lip gloss out of her pocket and applied it liberally. It was more distracting than it should have been. "So we're both just going to ignore what a terrible idea it is to storm the castle without Fezzik, huh?"

I flashed her my most dangerous grin. "Basically. Come on, Inigo."

At least, we reached the entrance, which was already oozing with eardrum-bursting techno. The bouncer in front of the felt barrier was a spindly bald man wearing a mesh shirt, leather pants, and combat boots. He spoke with a heavy Russian accent as he thrust out a hand to see our ID.

"What you come for, friends?"

Jordan flipped her hair in an expert way and tossed him a flirty smile as she gave him her card. "I hear this is where people go to get dirty. I'm feeling awful clean right now."

The Russian snorted and a smirk crawled its way across his lips. "You know what you getting into, little one?"

"Looking forward to it, handsome."

The Russian returned her ID. He glanced at me and the scowl returned in full force as he examined mine. "What you doing here, мальчик?"

I looped one arm around Jordan's shoulders and leaned her into my side. "Making sure she gets into as much trouble as possible."

"That is irresponsible, no?"

I let a predatory look slip across my features. "Not if I get to watch."

He eyed me for a moment and then handed my wallet back. He lifted the rope. "Enjoy."

We sidled past him. The entrance led down a short flight of stairs to the dark pit of sin and debauchery. Before we got there, Jordan tugged me down enough to whisper in my ear. "Nice line."

I grinned. "Nice hair toss."

Her laugh was swallowed by the thumping beat of a 3OH!3 song discussing why love was a word they'd never learn to pronounce. The dance floor was enormous—easily five hundred and fifty square feet—and on a raised square platform. There was a bar to the left already packed with people and tables were lined all around the outskirts of the floor. The DJ had a booth at the far wall, elevated so he could see everything. Green and purple lights shot through the crowd at random, momentarily illuminating the lewd acts commonly called dancing in the modern world. On the outside, it looked like every other joint in town, but it wasn't.

Every inch of this place made my very soul vibrate with rage. The demonic energy seeped over my pores and made me want to start a bar fight just because I was surrounded by fallen angels—by selfish, cruel monsters who preyed on the innocent. There were women in the booths along the right wall whose souls were being fed upon like they were nothing more than meat. It took all of my will power not to march over there and pull those siphoning bastards away from them. Free will and all that jazz.

Jordan must have felt my entire body go rigid. She slipped one arm around my waist and squeezed my side. I glanced down at her and she tugged me away from the stairwell. The movement helped snap me out of my momentary trance. I shook my head, took a deep breath, and focused on the task at hand.

We walked around the edge of the dance floor to check the place out. The women who passed by licked their lips and trailed their fingertips along my chest, hoping to sway me, but I kept walking. It was hard to see with the black lights and the constant strobe flashing, but there were a few hallways towards the right side of the club where they had rooms for private parties.

We were halfway there when a hand lashed out and yanked Jordan onto the dance floor. She only had time to cry out "Hey!" before the crowd swallowed her whole. I yelled her name, but it wasn't heard over the pounding music. I shoved my way through the writhing bodies, ignoring the touch of dozens of hands in some private places, searching desperately for her.

Luckily, I didn't have to go far. A small semi-circle opened up in the middle of the floor. I pushed through it. The unfortunate man who grabbed Jordan lay on his back with a bloody nose and Jordan was on top of him. She punched him twice more before I got my arms around her waist and hauled her off.

"Touch me again! I dare you!" she snarled as I carried her away, still fighting to get back over there and teach him a lesson. Normally, I'd have stood back and watched, but we had a job to do and little time left to do it.

I didn't let her go until we were off the dance floor and by then, she had calmed down a little. I set her down and noticed the edge of her lips was bloody.

"He hit you?" I asked, tilting her face so I could see. The cut was small, but she still winced as my thumb grazed her chin.

"No," she grumbled. "He kissed me. Tried to bite my lower lip off while he was at it. I'd have preferred a punch to that."

She lifted her hand to wipe the blood away, but that was when I noticed she'd gotten the attention of the demons around us. Blood had a sharp and alluring scent to them. It made them forget about being subtle and only feeding off of human emotion. She smelled like prey. I had to fix that or we'd be torn apart.

"Hold still," I whispered, and then bent towards her. She stiffened in my arms as I licked the corner of her lips. The blood was salty and acrid, but I made sure to get every bit of it. I wound my arms around her hips and pulled her fully against me, suppressing a shudder as her curves slid along my chest. She was warm and absurdly soft. I could see why they'd want her, and not just for her valuable Seer attributes.

I sent a harrowing glare at the small cluster of demons who had grouped behind us as the last drop of blood disappeared on my tongue. I laid a lingering kiss on her cheek and they finally broke up, returning to their various activities. The message was clear: *hands off*. They didn't always obey the rules, but they understood them.

I straightened up and cleared my throat, sending an apologetic look at her. "Sorry. Territorial issues."

"No shit," Jordan said, touching the spot where my mouth had been. "Guess I can cross 'have an archangel lick my face' off my bucket list."

I arched an eyebrow. "Should I even ask why it would be on there in the first place?"

She batted her eyelashes. "A girl doesn't kiss and tell. Now come on, Romeo, we've got work to do."

The dance floor vanished from sight as we made it to the other part of the club. There was a long, narrow hallway flocked with men and women waiting to get into the bathrooms. To our right was another stairway, but this one led up twelve steps to the second floor. Another bouncer with blond hair and enough muscles to make John Cena jealous stood there holding a clipboard. I pulled Jordan aside to the corner between the two hallways and leaned down so she could hear me.

"If we take out the guard, they'll get suspicious. How much cash do you have on you?"

She rifled through her wallet. "Just a twenty. What about you?"

"I've got forty. Not sure that's enough to bribe our way in."

"Maybe you should show him your boobs."

I frowned. "Not funny."

"Sorry, couldn't resist. Alright, follow my lead and don't freeze up on me."

"Freeze up?" I echoed, but then she caught my hand and dragged me around the corner before I could say anything. In that same handful of seconds, her entire demeanor changed. She added an extra sway to her hips that made certain areas jiggle with every step. She sashayed right over to the bouncer with me in tow and smiled wide.

"Hey there. How's your night going?"

His stony expression didn't change. "Sorry. Reserved rooms only. Take it elsewhere."

"Oh, come on," she said with a pout. "You've got to have just one itty bitty room that's not occupied."

"Not gonna happen."

She shook her head. "I don't think you understand."

She laid a hand on my chest and started rubbing one of my pectoral muscles in a slow circle. I had to force myself not to react because it felt pretty damn good. "You see, my friend and I were just having a very meaningful conversation before we got here and I'd really like to finish it."

"So rent a hotel room."

Jordan didn't let the utter rejection faze her. "Well, I may have forgotten to mention that I like having more than one…conversationalist. And you look like you have a very large…"

She flicked her eyes downward and then back up. Her smile stretched. "Vocabulary."

The bouncer didn't respond at first. He gave her a careful examination from head to toe and then inhaled deeply, as if smelling her. Something feral crawled into his blue eyes.

"A Seer, huh?"

"One of the only ones left. Not an opportunity you want to miss."

He licked his lips. "You do have a good point. People don't talk enough these days."

He opened the door to his immediate left and went inside for a moment. He returned with a key with a red plastic tag on it. "Second door to your right. Give me ten minutes and I'll be there."

"Looking forward to it," she purred as he stepped aside to let us pass. She led the way. I tried in vain to stare at everything but the view in front of me.

We reached the top and found ourselves in the middle of a wide split hallway. There were six doors on the right side and another six on the left. The dim lighting illuminated little else but the black numbers on each door. I couldn't hear anything from where we stood. Soundproof rooms. Bad news.

Jordan tucked the key in her pocket as we headed towards the right first. "Alright, what do you think?"

"I should stop underestimating you," I said, and then immediately realized that wasn't what she meant.

"Sorry, I mean, uh, you're going to have to focus your energy to try and sense Adira. If I do it, they'll be alerted to the fact that I'm an angel. After that, it's game over."

She chewed her bottom lip. "I've never done it in the presence of so many demons before. Will they be able to sense me too?"

"Not if they're distracted, which is what I'm betting on. Go ahead. I've got your back."

She nodded as if to steady herself and held out one hand, the palm perpendicular to the floor. She closed her eyes and slowly aimed her arm at each of the doors like a human compass. She considered a couple of them for around thirty seconds and then pointed to the left. "Down there. It's faint, but it's her."

I led her down the hall to the closed door she indicated—the third one from the end.

"Great. Now we just have to figure out how to get in, get out, and not get murdered," I said, smoothing my fingers through my hair. "Think your seduction trick would work on them?"

"Not en masse. It'd be way too suspicious."

"Wait. I think I've got an idea. But you have to trust me."

She eyed me. "Does it involve me getting naked?"

"No."

"Then quit flapping your gums and let's save her."

I almost smiled. That was Jordan. Always to the point. "One last thing. Bite your lip."

She raised an eyebrow. "We need to make it look like there was a struggle. You need to be bleeding."

~ 122 ~

"Roger that." She drew her bottom lip inward and bit down enough to reopen the cut. A couple dark droplets spilled down to her chin and she smeared them across her cheek to look like I'd popped her one. After she finished, I grabbed her by the collar and slammed my fist against the door several times.

Thomas Wingate opened it with an impatient glare. He had the door open enough that I could see into the room. Inside was a large rectangular lacquer table at the center surrounded by magenta-cushioned couches. Adira lay hogtied on her belly with a swollen black eye, a gag, and dried red stains on her forehead. Her cropped black hair stuck up in random tufts, sticky with sweat and blood. My soul boiled at the sight of one of my soldiers in such a state. The demons would pay dearly.

"Who are you?" Wingate spat.

I threw on a thick New York accent. "New guy. Hired me for security last night."

"The hell do you want?"

I hauled Jordan forward. "Guess what I caught sneakin' around? A Seer."

His brown eyes widened and then narrowed at her. He caught Jordan's face between his thick fingers and peered down at her, as if reading her energy. "I'll be damned. What's she doing here?"

"Think one of the angels might've sent her to find your girl in there. Thought you'd like to have a little fun with her too."

"Let go of me, you asshole!" Jordan growled, thrashing in my arms, but I held her still while Wingate contemplated my offer.

"Well, the pigeon's not squawking yet, so why not? Maybe we can carve this one up and guilt her into it." He held the door open and I carried Jordan in.

The room was big enough to fit no more than ten people, and there were four other guys in here with Wingate and Adira. The air stank of cigarette smoke and I realized why as I got closer. They'd taken off Adira's suit jacket, leaving her in a cobalt blue sleeveless shirt and a black skirt. The rich brown skin of her arms was dotted with several hideous burn marks that could've only come from lit cigarettes. Bastards.

Adira stiffened as she recognized me. I gave her an imperceptible nod as Wingate closed the door. The rope they'd tied her arms and legs with was so dark red it looked brown under the spotlights. They'd bound her with demon blood. Angels couldn't break bonds of that kind, not without a human or Seer's help.

"Gents, we have a guest. This little number is that Seer we've heard rumors about, the one who beat Belial at his own game."

Wingate picked up a still-lit cig that had been resting on a blue ash tray at the end of the table and sucked in a breath. I stood with my back to the wall opposite them and kept a firm grip on Jordan as I analyzed each man. Wingate had a Glock underneath his pinstriped suit, but the others were armed with knives. My guess was they hadn't been here long, because there wasn't a lot of blood or broken bones. Some demons liked to take their time. After all, they thought they'd won, so why rush?

"No shit," the black guy towards my right snorted. "Don't look like much."

"Yeah," I said. "But she's a fighter. Shoulda seen what happened when I grabbed her. She almost gave me a black eye."

The dark-haired demon next to him spoke up. "How'd she get past Dominic?"

"Told him she'd give him a BJ later."

Wingate laughed. "That asshole. Never thinking with the right body parts."

He stood in front of us and blew a gust of smoke into Jordan's face. She tried to turn her head, but he caught her chin yet again. "You got something to tell me, sweetheart?"

"Yeah. I'm gonna need some ear plugs if you're going to talk me to death. Nothing worse than a guy who likes the sound of his own voice."

Wingate chuckled. "Oh, we're gonna have a good time tonight. You're more fun than a barrel of monkeys, babe."

He nodded to me. "You search her for weapons or a wire yet?"

At last, a window of opportunity. "Not yet, boss."

"Go ahead. And do it slow. The boys and I like to watch."

A fresh round of sexist laughter went around the table as I shoved Jordan face first into the wall, though I made sure her head didn't hit it. When she didn't have her duster on, Jordan kept her pistol strapped to her ankle like a cop's backup weapon. I was tall enough that they wouldn't be able to see it with me in front of her. Six rounds and five demons. One miss and we'd be out of the frying pan and into the fire.

"Get your hands off me!" Jordan barked, continuing her rather admirable performance.

"Don't act like it's your first time, baby," I sneered, pinning her hands against the wall. "Now move again and I'll break your fingers."

She obeyed and I started to pat her down at the arms first. The demons let out a few nasty comments when my hands swept down her torso. One of them suggested I 'give her tits a quick fondle' and it took a lot of effort not to whirl around and rip his head off. Still, I didn't need them thinking I was a prude, so I pressed my face into her hair to mask what I was about to do.

"I'm going for your gun," I whispered in her ear. "Get ready."

"Got it," she murmured back.

I paused for one additional second.

"Sorry in advance."

I gave her backside a squeeze with both hands to appease the pigs behind me—who all guffawed heartily—and then patted down her legs. I sunk into a crouch and readied myself for the attack. I slipped the pistol from underneath the hemline of her jeans and rose upward. I pressed the cold metal against the small of her back. She reacted without hesitation.

I ducked as Jordan whirled around and shot at the demons closest to us. The black guy and the blond died instantly, but the third demon and fourth demons ducked beneath the table.

They came up with their knives drawn, but I was already waiting for them. I blocked the downward thrust of the blade with my forearm, kneed the attacker in the stomach, and then caught the knife as it fell from his grasp. I stabbed him in the chest and turned his body towards the other demon, who stabbed him between the shoulder blades. The first demon hit the floor in a bloody heap. I grabbed the other by the neck and I snapped it with a brusque movement. I turned to find Wingate and Jordan staring down the barrel at each other in a classic Mexican standoff.

"I should've known," Wingate growled, glaring at me. "You're too pretty to be a demon. Who are you?"

"Michael," I said through ragged breaths, flexing my hands open and closed. "You know that name. Drop the gun or you're next."

"You aren't in the position to be making demands. Your little girlfriend is fast, but she's not faster than me. I can pull the trigger before she even thinks about pulling hers. Call her off or she's dead."

"You kidnapped one of my people and now you're threatening someone I care very deeply about," I said slowly, letting him see the fury in my eyes. "Tread carefully, demon. You might not like what happens next."

"I'll take my chances." He glanced back at Jordan. "Shame to lose you. You're not bad for a Seer. Say goodbye to your angel."

"You first."

I lunged for Wingate as I saw his trigger finger twitch. I managed to grab him by the lapels and shove him against the wall. His shot missed Jordan by inches and the bullet hit one of the cushions in the couch beside her. He turned the gun on me, but I caught his wrist and twisted it to the side.

"Jordan!" I called out and she hit the floor as the gun went off several times, punching holes in the wall at random angles. I made sure none of them were close to where Adira lay on the table, but that couple of seconds cost me.

Wingate landed one hell of a punch to my diaphragm and all of the air whooshed out of my lungs. Dizziness turned him into a black-and-white blur in front of me, then I felt the hot muzzle of his Glock against my forehead. He fisted my hair and forced me onto my knees, his voice higher now with panic.

"Drop it!" he roared at Jordan. I could see out of my peripheral that she was on her knees, the gun pointed at him with just one bullet left. My body jerked and heaved with the effort to breath, but I was still too stunned to think past the pain.

"You know what your biggest mistake is in all of this?" Jordan asked in an unnervingly calm voice. "I'm not your main threat."

To my utter shock, she angled her arm towards Adira and pulled the trigger. The rope around the angel's wrists and feet fell slack. Her body uncurled from its painful position. She pulled off the gag and stood up with murder in her amber eyes.

Wingate gaped and shoved me aside, trying to aim at her, but he was far too late. Adira pinned him by the throat to the wall behind us and dug her fingers in until I heard a sharp crack. She dropped him and he fell like a broken marionette at her feet, his eyes glassy and open in death.

Jordan rushed over to me, rubbing my back in circles as I recovered. She glanced at the furious angel beside us. "You alright?"

Adira rolled her neck and winced as something popped. "I will be. I don't believe we've met, though."

Jordan offered her free hand. "Jordan Amador. Sorry we took so long."

She shook it. "Adira Mahmood. Sorry you had to risk your life for me."

Jordan smiled. "It happens."

She glanced at me once she noticed my breathing had stabilized. "You okay, tough guy?"

"Bruised ego," I rasped. "Nothing more."

The Seer rolled her eyes. "Naturally. Now how the hell do we get out of here? These rooms may be sound proof, but someone is bound to notice if we try to leave through the main exit."

"They brought me in through the back alley around the corner," Adira said. "If we hurry, we can make it before someone sees."

"Like we've ever been that lucky," I said with a grimace, standing up. Wingate may have been a thug, but he had one hell of an arm on him. Probably cracked a couple ribs, based on the intensity of the stabbing pain in my chest. "But it's the best plan we've got right now. Get ready."

Jordan scooped up Wingate's fallen Glock and checked the rounds while Adira and I both armed ourselves with the dead demons' knives. I flattened myself against the door and mouthed that I'd count down from three.

On cue, I opened the door, knife raised and ready. Empty hallway. Maybe fortune had found herself a little smirk tonight. I motioned for Adira to lead the way towards the back entrance while I brought up the rear and we crept as quietly as possible down the hallway, straining to hear any signs of movement. The closed door directly across from the stairwell inched closer.

"Figures," a familiar male voice spoke from behind us.

I whirled to see Dominic the bouncer pointing a .45 at my head with a grim smirk on his lips.

"I thought you two had a weird vibe coming off you. It's too bad."

His eyes slid to Jordan, who stood directly behind me. "You got one sweet little—"

"Do not finish that sentence," I said in a low voice.

He fell silent and then bared his teeth. "Ass."

I reversed the knife in my hand and threw it straight into his left eye. He died instantly. However, his heavy frame stumbled backwards first and then went tumbling down the steps. *Shit!*

As soon as he hit the bottom, someone screamed.

"Cheese it!" Jordan shouted, and the three of us bolted for the door. Adira kicked it open and we raced down the twisted staircase that led out of the club. The cool night air greeted us as we hit the alley, enclosed on both sides by brick. I heard the faint hammering of footsteps behind us and poured on my agility to catch up with Adira.

"Take Jordan and head as far away from here as you can get. I'll hold them off."

"What?" Jordan demanded. "I'm not leaving you here!"

We skidded to a stop at the edge of the alley — to the left, a dead end and the street to our right. I could bottleneck the demons here until the girls were safe.

"She's right," Adira said with a stubborn look matching Jordan's. "Come with us."

I shook my head. "You'll need a head start. Go. That's an order, soldier."

Adira clenched her jaw and cursed in Latin under her breath. She looped an arm around Jordan's waist and lifted her as if she weighed no more than a child.

"No, wait! Michael, you jackass!" Jordan struggled, but Adira carried her off around the corner.

I faced the alley in front of me and held my arm straight up. The clouds in the night sky gathered into a thick mass and thunder rumbled. Seconds later, my sword, Celeste, came flying down to meet my open hand.

The back door swung wide and demons — male and female alike — poured out of it with bloodlust in their eyes. I shrugged out of my leather jacket, tossed it aside, and rolled one shoulder. A fearsome grin overtook my features before I could help it.

"Evening, friends. Who's first?"

The next thing I remembered was the touch of someone's fingers on my cheeks. Warm. Delicate. Too bad they were shaking my head and causing pain to shoot through my brain like icy spikes.

I groaned and attempted to open my eyes. I was successful on the second try. Colors melted and bled together in a kaleidoscope. Eventually, the hazy mess cleared and I realized I was still in the alley, only horizontal and covered in blood. Jordan was on her knees beside me, kneeling among the dozens of eviscerated demons.

She let out a relieved sigh when she saw my eyes open. "You stubborn bastard."

"What are you doing here?" I muttered, trying to glare, but I was too damn tired. "I told you to run."

"I did," she said tartly. "I also came back with help. Gabriel is on his way to retrieve your big stupid ass."

"Don't need help. I'm fine."

"Can you even sit up?"

I thought about it. My entire body felt like one aching knot. I had barely any sensation in my extremities aside from sharp pain. It wasn't surprising. I'd fought at least thirty demons by myself.

"…eventually, yeah."

She chuckled and there was an echo of something fragile in it. "Hard ass."

I heard footsteps approaching. The girls were safe. Evil had been vanquished. Time for this angel to take a little nap. I let my eyelids drop closed as I drifted off once more.

"Stop thinking about my butt, you pervert."

Her full lips pressed against my forehead. Or maybe I dreamt that part.

A couple hours later, I was back to normal. Jordan and Adira naturally couldn't call the cops, considering the fact that we'd killed more than a few people, so they relocated me to Adira's home on the other side of Albany. The demons wouldn't bother trying to call the authorities on us either because it would bring the club under investigation. They'd lick their wounds and plot their revenge. Just as well. We'd be ready for that day too.

"That should do it," Gabriel said with a sigh, straightening up—which was quite the task for him at six-foot-six—and wiping his hands with a fresh towel after healing me. Of the two of us, he was much fairer, with wintry blue eyes and golden-blond hair that was always perfectly gelled. Raphael was the archangel of healing, but Gabriel shared his ability to put me at ease even in the worst of times.

I sat on the edge of Adira's bed and it was squishy and comfortable. Probably a Tempur-Pedic. Sleep sounded like an excellent idea, but I'd have to go home for that.

Adira's wounds were already healed, to my relief. She offered me her hand. "I am indebted to you, Commander."

I shook it. "Don't be. Just wish we'd gotten there sooner."

She smiled. "You did all that you could. Besides, I am impressed. You and the Seer work well together. I see why you left your post in Heaven for her."

I cleared my throat and avoided her affectionate gaze. "I wouldn't put it that way."

"I'm sure you wouldn't," Gabriel said with a sly look, and I glared at him.

Adira laughed. It was light and musical. I was happy to hear it. "Be that as it may, thank you for your help. I'll make you some tea as my show of appreciation."

She gave Gabriel a fond pat on the shoulder on her way out. He regarded me with a thoughtful look after she left. "So you took Jordan with you."

"Turned out to be a good idea. It would have been harder to get in without her."

"Do you plan to make a habit out of it?"

I frowned. "Not if I can help it. The only reason I said yes is because I knew I could protect her. Plus, she was a valuable asset."

He crossed his arms. "Are you sure of that, brother?"

I had known him for ages. There was something hidden in his tone. "What are you really asking me, Gabriel?"

"She found you buried beneath a pile of dead bodies. She thought she'd lost you. I have not seen her so upset in a long while. Perhaps these kinds of missions are the ones we should keep between us."

I leaned my arms on my knees and stared at the fuzzy tan carpet. "It's the nature of the beast. She's a Seer. She'll only see more violence in her lifetime, not less."

He rested a hand on my shoulder. "I know. But I would caution you to be more careful. Jordan has seen someone she cared about die right in front of her. I would not want her to relive the experience if at all possible. Please consider that."

I opened my mouth to reply, but then Jordan opened the door. She had a hilariously large blueberry muffin in one hand that made me salivate on sight.

"Hey," she said, walking over. "How're you feeling?"

"Hungry."

"Figured as much. Here." I took the biggest bite possible and nearly fainted from the sweet taste. Otis Spunkmeyer must be in league with Satan. These things were unreal.

She licked a few crumbs from her fingertips and then nudged Gabriel when she noticed his somber expression. "What's up? Did I interrupt something?"

"No, not at all, my dear. Are you sure you're alright?"

"Healthy as a horse. Thanks for coming to the rescue."

"For you? Always." He kissed her forehead and left the two of us alone.

Jordan watched me devour the muffin in minutes before speaking. "So what happened back there?"

"Hmm?" I said in between licking my lips.

She sank down next to me onto the plush mattress. "Why didn't you want me to stay with you? I could have helped."

"You also could have gotten dead."

"That was my choice."

I shut my eyes for a moment. "I had it handled. It would've been a stupid thing for you to lose your life over—"

"And who says I would have lost my life? You?"

I glared. "You forget the part where I've been alive for literally thousands of years. I can tell the outcome of most events, even if it hurts your feelings."

"My feelings," she said with an indignant snort. "This is not about my feelings. Do you think I'm a capable adult, Michael?"

"Of course I do."

"Then don't treat me like a child. I'm your friend. If I'm your backup, you don't cut me out of the final boss battle."

"It's not that simple."

"Because?"

Words dried up in my mouth. I swallowed. It hurt. She kept staring expectantly at me, but nothing came out so I just looked at the floor.

She sighed. "Fine. If you want to brood, then let me get out of your way." Jordan stood up and walked to the door.

"I watched you die."

She froze. Didn't turn around. I didn't mind since I wasn't sure what my face looked like right now. "You were gone, Jordan. For almost a day until I asked Father to restore your life. I've seen people die before, but never someone I knew the way I know you. I can't…do that again. I made a judgment call. I thought it was the right one, but it's not. It's the one I needed. It's been over a month since that day and I still feel like I have to atone for what I let happen to you."

Slowly, she faced me. "You didn't let anything happen to me, Michael. It was Belial. He's the one to blame for my death, not you. You should be smart enough to know that."

A bitter chuckle spilled out of my mouth. "Not sure if you've noticed, but I'm not exactly Einstein."

She sat next to me again and bumped my shoulder so I'd look at her. "All I want is for you to believe in me. That's it. Everything else will fall into place on its own, okay? No more heroics."

She held out her hand. "Deal?"

I took it. "Deal."

"Look on the bright side. At least you have something to write about now."

I chuckled. "Yep. I'm gonna call it 'Murder at the Disco.'"

"It'll be on the Top Ten charts by the end of the year."

"No doubt."

SLOTH III

"Do I *have* to come out?"

"Yes."

"Seriously?"

"Yes."

I heard a haggard sigh from the other side of Jordan's closed bedroom door. "Fine, but just so you know, this is ruining a perfectly good night. I was going to stay in bed in my underwear eating Chinese takeout."

I adjusted my maroon tie in the reflection of the microwave. "Thanks for that mental image."

"Shut up. I hate you."

"Uh-huh." At this point, the word 'hate' didn't mean much coming from her. Jordan disliked a lot of things, and I was occasionally on that list for pushing her to do stuff she wouldn't normally do. Like tonight, for instance. The angels in the Albany area were having what amounted to a staff meeting at a dining hall downtown. Black tie affair. Gabriel insisted that I bring Jordan along to get the other angels acquainted with her. I hadn't told her there was a bit of a hidden agenda. Some of the angels felt resentful that I wasn't up in Heaven giving out orders like I used to and couldn't understand why I was in the trenches, so to speak.

The bedroom door opened. I glanced over, expecting the sour scowl on her face, but not the effect her gown would have on me.

Gabriel had very kindly bought her a strapless silk dress the color of freshly fallen snow. Fringes of red lace lined the edge of the bodice and the hem. A slit went up the right side that ended a couple inches above her knee, revealing a nice line of her leg without giving it all away. He'd also given her the jewelry to match—bright red bracelets and earrings that jingled when she moved. Her black hair fell around her shoulders, contrasting wonderfully with her brown skin and the white of the dress. I wouldn't have recognized her if not for the frown and the barest glimpse of a bandage over the healing wound on her chest.

She threw up her hands, glaring. "I look ridiculous."

"That is…" I cleared my throat, forcing my gaze away from her terribly distracting hourglass figure. "Not the word I'd use."

Jordan rolled her eyes and stomped past me, sending sharp clicks echoing through the room with her heels. "Why can't you angels just meet in a church or something? What's with the fancy get up if it's only a meeting to play catch-up on recent events?"

"You have to understand that the angels come from Heaven, where everything is literally perfection," I said, texting Gabriel to let him know we were on our way out. "Down here, it's impossible to replicate, so they do the best they can. That's why Gabriel is always so extravagant in anything he does. He's never known otherwise."

"Hmph," she replied, tossing her phone and keys into the small purse that had come with the dress. "I can teach them a thing or two about poverty if given the chance."

I shook my head, unable to resist a smile. All that beauty wrapped around all that cynicism. I'd never understand it. "Are you cranky because you're not getting Chinese or are you just nervous?"

She froze, blinking rapidly at me. "I'm not nervous."

The answer came so quickly I knew she was lying. I sighed. "It's perfectly fine if you are."

Jordan avoided my gaze as she looped her stole around her shoulders. "I'm not nervous. I'm just…uncomfortable wearing a dress that costs more than my rent."

I offered her my arm. "Well, get over it, Amador. You look beautiful."

She studied me for a moment or two, as if trying to determine if I meant the comment. Then she settled one hand on the inside of my bicep. "Fine. But you're still getting me Chinese on the way home."

I chuckled as I led her to the door. "Yes, ma'am."

We caught a cab to the dining hall the angels had rented for the night. The attendance would be moderate this time around—no more than twenty guests, not including us. It was a private affair, so there was no chance of any humans stumbling in and finding out about us. They'd hired a couple bouncers to ensure no party crashers broke in.

Jordan squeezed my arm a bit when we came up to the closed doors guarded by two gargantuan dark-haired men in tuxedos with links in their ears. They nodded to me, but then tossed her suspicious looks.

"What's with the girl?" the one on the right growled.

"She's my guest. This is Jordan Amador."

They exchanged looks. "The Seer?"

"Yes."

The guy on the left snorted, his eyes wandering over her from head to toe. "Not what I expected, but…nice to finally meet you, Miss Amador."

"Ditto," she said. "And my eyes are up here."

She continued through the doors without another word. First impressions, Amador style. Tonight was definitely going to be interesting.

The dining hall could hold over a hundred people easy. The floors were polished hardwood and the seven round tables draped in white cloth. Two bars laden with food lined either side of the walls. I even spotted a chocolate fountain at the dessert table next to the drinks.

The entertainment for the night was a small orchestra at the head of the room. I counted eight total members — four violins, three violas, and a cello. The conductor's arms waved back and forth to the soothing music. All this for a staff meeting. I couldn't decide if it was ludicrous or simply amusing.

"Do we have assigned seating?" Jordan asked, her eyes a bit wide as she took it all in.

"Not really," I said, scanning the crowd for Gabriel. I spotted him near the fruit basket and gently tugged her along with me.

"Gabe," I said, once we were within earshot.

He turned and smiled wide with delight. His suit was pure white with a gold tie and robins-egg blue shirt beneath it. He put down his small plate and shook my hand. "There you are. I was beginning to worry you wouldn't show."

I sent a sly glance at Jordan. "Not for lack of trying."

She rolled her eyes at me and greeted him. "Evening, Gabe. You look great."

He caught both of her hands, spreading her arms so he could see the overall effect of the dress. "You are a vision of loveliness, Jordan. Why do you not dress like this all the time?"

"Slide me some of those millions of yours and I will."

Gabriel laughed and kissed her cheek. "I shall see what I can do. In the meantime, please indulge yourself in some of this delectable food. Our table is right up front. I'll be there shortly after I make my rounds."

He nodded to us, retrieved his plate of goodies, and headed towards a cluster of angels that gathered near the punch bowl. Jordan watched him go with a fond look and then sighed as her gaze returned to the food table.

"I'm wearing white. I'm too scared to eat anything."

"That's never stopped you before."

She whacked me in the shoulder. "I'll have you know some men like a girl with a healthy appetite."

I picked up one of the chocolate-covered strawberries and waved it in front of her teasingly. "Healthy isn't in your vocabulary, last time I checked."

She caught my hand and bit into the fruit. A droplet of juice slid down the corner of her lips, already red with lipstick that matched the dress. I couldn't focus on anything else for a good three seconds. She sent me a flirty smile and winked before taking the fruit out of my hand.

"Check again, archangel."

With that, she left my side and got herself a plate while I tugged at my collar and wondered when it had suddenly gotten so hot in here.

"Michael."

I jumped at the sound of my name, turning to see a large black man wearing a charcoal grey suit and a Japanese woman in a periwinkle blue dress. I sifted through my memory banks until I recalled their names and positions. Marcus was a surgeon at St. Peter's Hospital while Ling was a homicide detective.

"Marcus, Ling, how are you?" They both shook my hand respectively.

"Good to see you, Commander," Marcus said in his booming voice. "Odd, but good."

"How have you been keeping?" Ling asked.

"Well," I said, tucking my hands in my pockets. "Some trouble here and there, but nothing I can't handle."

"I've heard as much," she said, her brown eyes wandering over to Jordan, who appeared to be out of earshot. "Is that the Seer?"

"Yes, that's Jordan."

Ling crossed her arms. "That was some impressive work she did killing Mulciber. Have you been training her?"

"Yeah. She's extremely competent and capable. That's why I wanted her to get acquainted with the local angels. Might come in handy someday."

"I see," Marcus said. "We heard about that mess with Adira, and then Jean Winters sending an assassin after you. A lot of trouble has been brewing this past month. Think it's all related?"

"I wouldn't be surprised."

"What's his current status?"

"He's gone into hiding." I couldn't disguise the growing anger and bitterness in my words. "We've got a warrant for his arrest out, but the hit-woman said he was going to fake his own death and find a new body. They interrogated the assassin, but nothing's come of it yet. Not surprising."

Marcus frowned. "You didn't interrogate her first?"

I held his gaze. "She shot me in the chest six times. It would've been unwise to do so."

Jordan returned from the food table, greeting the two angels. "Hi. I'm Jordan. Sorry, didn't mean to interrupt."

The angels nodded to her, but I noticed their smiles were frosty. "Nice to meet you. If you'll excuse us."

They retreated toward another couple not far away. Jordan popped a red grape into her mouth as she watched them leave. "Wow. Didn't think I could muck things up that quickly. Think I broke my record."

"Relax," I said, beckoning her towards our table. "Some angels are just uptight."

I pulled out her chair and she sat, allowing me to push her up to the table for once. Most of the time, she shooed me away from doing gentlemanly things because it made her feel like I was her boyfriend. Her words, mind you.

"Or they're just protective of their leader."

I couldn't stop surprise from stealing across my face. Jordan shook her head. "I'm not an idiot, Michael. I know there's some tension going on in the ranks. Makes sense. These people don't know me, and to them, it might seem like I'm corrupting you or something."

I offered her a sheepish look after I took my seat. "Are you mad?"

"No. You do a lot of things that annoy me, but at least this makes sense. I need to know what kind of world I'm a part of now. I'm glad you're trying to teach me."

She paused. "But I still don't like this dress."

I smiled. "Fair enough."

"I have to admit, though, it's not a bad unnecessary shindig. Though the music could use some work. That cello on the right is nowhere near tuned properly."

I glanced at the tall, thin cello player with slicked back hair and spider-like fingers. "How the hell would you know that?"

"My ex listened to classical music when he studied. Said it helped him concentrate. We went to a few live performances too." She made a point not to look at me as she revealed this information. Jordan rarely spoke of her past relationship. I still didn't know much about Terrell Molding other than his occupation and his ideals. I tried not to pry on a consistent basis since it made her act squirrely, but I did wonder what their dynamic had been like. A more selfish part of my brain wanted to know if he was anything like me, but I ignored it.

Marcus and Ling joined our table a moment later, and then Gabriel stepped up to the podium placed about ten feet away. The orchestra played its final notes and went silent. The crowd gave them a round of applause and then my brother spoke.

"Good evening, ladies and gentlemen. I'd like to thank you for joining us tonight. I know many of you have busy schedules, so it warms my heart to see you all. We have a lot on the roster tonight in terms of updates. I shall try to get the boring items out of the way as soon as possible."

A few giggles sounded throughout the room. He then launched into the usual housekeeping kind of stuff for the angels in the area—crime trends, intel on the demon nests, new weapons specialists to fine-tune our equipment, changes in the ranks of heaven's army, and recent activity in the demon community. After a certain point, my eyes began to glaze over, but I noticed Jordan paid rapt attention, her eyes bright with interest.

Half an hour crept by before Gabriel wrapped up. "Now then, we will have a little departure from the usual. Most of you are already aware that the Commander is in our midst. He's going to say a few words on his experience these past couple weeks. Welcome him, would you?"

Gabriel stepped aside as I came up to the podium amid the applause. By now, the orchestra players had vacated their seats to partake in the buffet, leaving me alone in front of the many eyes. I adjusted the mic down to my height and cleared my throat.

"Evening, folks. Good to see you out and about. I just wanted to clear the air a bit since I know the rumor mill has been churning pretty hard lately."

I took a deep breath. "Not long ago, the archdemon Belial and I fought over the Spear of Longinus. He was able to wipe my existence from history until I met a Seer named Jordan Amador, who helped me recover my memories and set everything back the way it was."

I snuck a look at Jordan, who very meekly sipped her white grape juice and avoided my gaze. Typical.

"I'm sure you all noticed the change and it was deeply disconcerting to know the Spear held that much power. Rest assured, it's been returned to Heaven and is out of anyone's hands for the rest of eternity. On a note closer to home, I've seen a lot of dangerous activity in Albany lately. Kidnappings, soul-trafficking, murders, the works. They are getting bolder. I know each and every one of you is doing your job and I thank you for it, but I must caution you to watch your backs. It has been a long time since I spent my days on Earth, and now I see why it's necessary for me to be back. Times are changing. The people we protect need us now more than ever. This war of ours gets bloodier by the day, but we must remember what's important."

I paused as I heard a phantom sound out of my right ear. Something high pitched, almost like when someone turned on a television without turning on the cable box—a whine that would be nigh-inaudible to anyone but me. Frowning, I glanced aside near the abandoned instruments of the orchestra. Earlier, Jordan said something about a cello out of tune. Then it hit me.

"Everyone down!" I shouted as I dove for Jordan. I had just enough time to pull her into my arms and sprout my wings before the bomb went off.

The explosion flash-fried the length of my spine and the base of my neck, reducing the back of my suit to tatters. My wings acted as a shield to the fire, but I felt an entire layer of feathers burn right off. The sound of the concussive blast deafened me and left a piercing ringing in my perforated eardrums instead. Jordan's nails dug into my chest as she hugged me to her, shaking violently after the explosion subsided.

Slowly, I lifted my head enough to see if she'd been harmed. "Are you okay?"

Jordan nodded, and I had to read her lips to understand her as she asked the same of me.

"I'll be alright."

I kept my arms around her waist, pulling her up with me as I stood and retracted my wings from around us to survey the damage.

Thankfully, most of the angels heard my warning. Many of them were face down on the floor with their wings out, shielding them. Smoke choked the air as much as the stench of burnt feathers and furniture. Tables and chairs were overturned and smoldering. The instruments from the orchestra had been vaporized on the spot, leaving nothing but streaks of ash from the blast site. Someone had gone through a lot of trouble hiding that bomb, and I was damn sure going to figure out who.

I closed my eyes and concentrated on my energy, healing my ears. A wave of sounds hit me—coughing, moaning, and broken pieces of the ceiling hitting the hardwood floor. I laid my hands on the either side of Jordan's face and healed her ears as well.

"Check for pulses and see who's not moving," I told her. I spotted the golden feathers belonging to my brother beneath a charred broken half of our table. I tossed it aside and found him sprawled on his side, his once glorious white suit torn asunder and smudged with ash.

I hooked one arm beneath Gabriel's broad back and helped him sit up. "Are you alright, brother?"

He coughed deeply into his hand and blood spotted his palm. Damn it. "I shall…live. Is Jordan—"

"She's okay."

He tried to stand, but his legs crumpled beneath him. I helped him out of the remains of his suit jacket and winced as I saw the many bloody spots of shrapnel in his chest and side. "Try not to move. You seem to have gotten the worst of it."

Gabriel grimaced, skimming his fingertips over the lacerations. "My popularity is an awful burden sometimes."

I started to lay my hand on the worst of the wounds, but he shook his head and pointed towards the rest of the room. "Help the others. I'll be fine. Go."

I didn't believe him, and he probably didn't either, but I did as he told me. Five of the angels in attendance were unconscious, and one was in critical condition. I gave him CPR until the ambulance arrived and the cops not long after them. I helped get everyone out of the dining hall and into the good hands of angelic doctors before addressing the most important thing of all: who the hell tried to kill us and how had he gotten that bomb into the hall?

I told the cops my theory about the bomb being hidden inside the cello. The majority of the orchestra members—who I later found out were humans in-the-know, as we called them—were just as shocked as we were at the bombing, but unsurprisingly, the cello player was nowhere to be found. The cops took the entire group into custody and promised to put out an APB on the cellist before they left to interrogate them.

I found out the staff meeting had been organized by Josie, an angel who worked as a professional decorator, and she'd been recommended this group by a client. I got a background check on the client, but she didn't have any priors. It seemed like a dead end until I went through her financial history and found a chilling fact.

She had once hired Lanning and Holmes for a case.

Jean Winters' law firm.

Son of a bitch.

I found Jordan in the back of an ambulance using an O2 machine. The EMTs had placed a blanket around her shoulders, and I could see her trembling just a bit as I approached. Her eyes widened as she saw me for the first time in nearly an hour.

My suit pants were still somewhat intact, but I'd removed my shredded dress shirt long ago. The fact that my entire spine was numb probably meant I had third degree burns. The skin on my biceps, shoulders, and elbows was mottled red and pink underneath a layer of ash. I probably looked like fifteen different kinds of hell, and couldn't have cared less about it.

She lowered the mask when I was within earshot. "Found something?"

"Yeah," I said, and couldn't hide the sheer wrath in my tone. "I need you to do something for me."

"Anything," she said automatically.

"Stay with Gabriel tonight. Take him with you to your apartment or stay at his place. I've got to track down this bastard and feed him his own dick."

"The cellist?"

"He's got it coming, but he isn't the cause. It was Winters."

She stilled for a moment. "You're sure?"

"Damn sure."

"Can you handle him alone?"

I let out an ugly laugh. She shivered, as if it had touched her. "Handle is a mild way of putting it."

"And you don't need me with you." The last part came out the tiniest bit vulnerable, and it was statement more than a question.

I met her eyes for a long moment, reading the hesitance in them. "I can't risk it. He resorted to a bomb. There's no telling what depths he'll sink to if I don't stop him. What I've got to do...it won't be pretty. I don't want you around for it. It has nothing to do with you not being strong enough. You are, but...there are sides to me that you may not like, Jordan. Bad sides. I still want your friendship when this is over, so please, just stay with Gabriel for now."

She nodded. "You saved my life again."

I shrugged. "I owed you."

She smiled, and it was watery around the edges. "Go kick his ass."

"Will do."

I hesitated, wanting to give her some sign of reassurance, but it was hard enough not simply scooping her up in my arms. If she hadn't heard that out-of-tune cello, she might not be here to encourage me to kill the shit out of Jean Winters. It scared me to think she could have been gone just that fast, and I could have been holding her cold and lifeless in my arms again. I cared entirely too much about this girl I'd known for only a month.

To hell with it. Life was too damn short.

I held out my hand. She gave me hers. I kissed her knuckles, briefly, and squeezed her fingers before letting go. Then I squared my shoulders, turned, and went hunting.

Tracking the cellist was difficult, but not impossible. I predicted he'd been slipped into the group at the last minute as a replacement — which the conductor corroborated — and had been paid handsomely to remote-detonate the bomb once I was in close range. Charles McKenzie didn't have a record, but I suspected his current identity was fake. No one hired an amateur for an operation like this one. He was a professional.

Most career criminals knew how to avoid capture soon after the crime. Preparing an inconspicuous escape route was usually a good idea if they didn't have an identity to worry about, or were working as an out-of-town gun-for-hire. With twenty angels in attendance, word for his capture would get around quickly. He'd probably opt for ground transportation since airports had so many cameras.

I caught a break when one of Ling's people called and told me the last place he'd been seen prior to the meeting was at a gas station. He gave me the make and model of the car, which was confirmed with one of the witnesses on the street who said she saw him fleeing the scene right after the explosion. The cellist accounted for a lot of things, but he didn't consider what the streets of Albany looked like on a weeknight. A couple angels found him sandwiched in gridlock traffic thirteen miles from the dining hall, on his way to the interstate.

McKenzie put up a decent fight, but the angels overwhelmed him and brought him to me. I located a quaint little basement specifically reserved for interrogations and instructed them to meet me there.

When I came in, he was duct-taped to a chair by the wrists, ankles, and midsection, along with some over his mouth. Sweat plastered his scraggly black hair to his face.

He breathed in great gulps, but the glare he bestowed on me meant he was angry, not scared. Not yet, anyway.

"He say anything about the bombing?" I asked.

"No, sir. Haven't heard a peep since we grabbed him."

I nodded towards the door. "Thanks for your help. I've got it from here."

They left, shutting the door behind them. I locked it and dragged up a chair from next to the table. The house had been foreclosed and was owned by the bank. Bare wooden walls, dusty floor, and empty space except for the two of us and a workman's table with a buzzsaw on it. If McKenzie were a demon, I'd have populated the stable with wickedly sharp knives, holy water, and some crosses, but he was human. It wouldn't take much to break him.

I turned the chair backwards and sat in it with my legs spread, settling my forearms on it. Pins and needles stung up and down my arms still. I hadn't the time to heal my wounds completely, but I'd healed enough to function. I'd swung by a department store for clothes and decided to go for the intimidating colors: black dress shirt, grey slacks, and boots.

"I'd introduce myself, but I'm pretty sure you know my name."

McKenzie's brow furrowed beneath his tangled locks. "Don't play dumb. Demons haven't tried an assassination like that in years. It's not a coincidence. We've already linked you to Jean Winters through one of the past clients at his firm. When we're done here, you're going into police custody. That'll be the end of your story."

I leaned forward a bit. "But we're not at the end of your story. We're in the middle. I don't care about your past indiscretions. I'm sure you'll pay for them soon enough. I want Winters. You're going to give me anything and everything I ask about him, or I'm going to repaint the basement walls with your bodily fluids. Understand?"

He continued glaring. I stripped half of the duct tape away, leaving it dangle awkwardly to one side like he'd grown a tail on his face.

McKenzie licked his chapped lips. "I know where Winters is."

He took a reedy breath. "All you have to do is stick your head up your ass and you'll find him."

I pressed the duct tape across his mouth. Then I caught his first finger and jammed it all the way back until I heard the muscles pop in his hand. He screamed—high pitched like a female soprano singer—through the duct tape. I stopped just short of breaking the digit and let him catch his breath.

"That was less than five percent of my strength," I said in my most lifeless voice. "If you ever want to use that cello again, you should answer truthfully."

I peeled the tape back yet again. "Go fuck yourself, pretty boy."

A muscle in my jaw twitched. "You know, I really don't like that moniker."

I stood and went over to the workman's table. The buzzsaw sat there, cleaned and oiled, ready to be used. The place still had power, so I plugged it in and gave it a quick whirl just to see the look on McKenzie's face. He went so pale I thought he'd faint.

"The average demon can withstand having their arms and legs removed if it's done with a manmade instrument," I said, walking towards him. "It's usually the genitals that do them in. Some of them just throw in the towel and descend back to Hell because it's better than getting their junk lopped off."

I revved the buzzsaw once, just a couple inches from his cheek. The air from the blades ruffled his hair. He flinched, trying to lean away from them. "But you're not a demon, McKenzie. I don't have all damn night. Answer my question, or you'll be the world's greatest one-armed cellist. Or, if you prefer, the world's greatest eunuch cellist."

"Y-You can't do this to me!" he stammered, eyes wide. "You're an angel! That'd be a sin."

"You bombed a room full of God's own soldiers. I'm not sinning. I'm avenging."

I flipped the saw on and inched toward his spread legs. "Alright, stop, just stop it! I don't know where he is, but I can give you the account he used to wire me the money!"

I edged away from his crotch. "Smart man. Stay put while I get a pen."

I dropped the buzzsaw into his lap just for good measure, though I turned it off. The little shriek he made almost improved my mood.

It had crept up on eleven o'clock by the time I reached the office of the new-and-improved Jean Winters. His current alias was of no consequence. Every demon and angel had their own unique energy signature. Winters' reminded me of the slime that floated to the surface of a pond—thick, slick, and saturating everything it touched with muck.

"So. Here we are yet again." Winters sat in a comically large leather chair. The plaque on his desk read Brock Parker. Fitting, considering he had assumed the position of editor-in-chief at a local newspaper with the word 'Daily' in the title.

The office could have fit about eight of the cubicles on the other side of the closed door. He had a 44-inch plasma flat-screen TV, a mini-fridge, microwave, and couch on one side, and a mammoth bookshelf on the opposite wall. Grey carpet. Great view of the city skyline behind him. All in all, he seemed to be doing well for himself…until tonight.

The man himself picked a different body — that of a gentleman in his early fifties. Square jaw, dimples in his cheeks, big white teeth, and a lanky musculature. Grey touched his temples on either side of his sandy brown hair and he had just enough stubble to appear rugged. I instantly thought of Dr. Perry Cox if he'd gone to the Dark Side.

Winters spread his arms in a welcoming gesture. "You caught up to me faster than I predicted. I take it you entertained my guests well?"

"You could say that," I said, resting one hand on the hilt of my sword. It was long past late hours at this office, so I'd had enough cover to summon Celeste. I made a promise to run this bastard through myself. I was aching to keep it.

"Glad to hear it. So what is your plan, Commander?"

A smirk slipped across my lips. "I think we already discussed that at the restaurant a week ago."

"You'll kill me here? With cameras and no possible way to escape without leaving evidence? Quite bold, wouldn't you say?"

I walked toward him with a steady, determined pace. "One of the perks of being friends with cops is that they can clean up the mess better than anyone else. They know what to look for, after all."

He stood, running his ringed fingers along the edge of his desk as he walked around it. "I suppose I could make some grand speech about how your little Seer will die if I die, but we both know it will change nothing. You are a man of your word, archangel. You'd sooner commit *seppuku* than not fulfill a promise of revenge."

"Not revenge," I snarled. "Justice. If you have a problem, you come after me. Only a coward would target the innocent. If that's not enough, you couldn't even summon the balls to kill her yourself."

"I don't like to get my hands dirty."

"They look plenty filthy to me."

"Spare me the lecture, boy. Your ideals are antiquated. Killing you has nothing to do with destroying your body. Your soul, however, has somehow found its way inside the body of that waitress you're protecting. I will unravel it thread by thread."

"Your last words." I unsheathed my sword and darted for him.

He reached beneath the edge of his desk and withdrew a .357 Magnum, firing without hesitation. I managed to dodge the first four bullets and brought my sword up to deflect the others as I closed in. The shots vibrated down the blade, into the hilt, and back up my arm. He emptied the chambers by the time I was within arms' length.

I slashed at him, aiming for his head, but he ducked and smashed the butt of the gun into my nose hard enough to break it. I ignored the pain and grabbed his right wrist as it skimmed past my face. I twisted his arm out in front of me and chopped off his hand.

Winters screamed and stumbled backwards, splattering a crooked line of blood across the carpet. His blue eyes bulged nearly out of his skull. Saliva frothed from either side of his lips as if he'd gone rabid with rage. "You bastard!"

I spit out a mouthful of blood. "I think you misspoke, demon. I do, in fact, have a father."

He reached inside his pocket and then flicked his wrist, revealing a switchblade. He let the spurting blood from his severed arm coat the blade, turning it from a manmade weapon into one that could actually kill me, and then lunged.

Winters' movements were damn near too fast to follow. He aimed for my throat, my chest, my sword arm, hoping to catch me off-guard. I stayed defensive, blocking, parrying, searching for my opening. He slung his right arm at my face, trying to blind me with his own blood, but I whirled to the side instead.

He anticipated my dodge and tripped me up, riding my body down onto the floor. I held the flat of my blade at his forearm and strained to hold him off as he bore down. The blade inched closer to my throat, dripping hot blood onto my Adam's apple.

"Give it up, Michael. It doesn't matter if you win this day or the next. My kind is destined to wipe the human vermin from this world. It's inevitable. All you're doing is putting out fires, and they will consume you no matter how hard you try."

"Poor choice of words, old man."

I reached into my pocket and broke a vial of holy oil across the right side of his face.

Winters roared in pain as the purified oil ate right through his skin like acid, rolling aside and clawing at it with his remaining hand. The acrid stench of burning flesh quickly filled the room as he rolled around in pure agony, cursing me with every labored breath. I stood up and watched it melt clean through to the bone, leaving him twitching on the floor in shock.

I popped open the second vial of holy oil I brought with me and dumped it on his chest. It soaked through his thousand-dollar dress shirt and began to scald the demonic flesh beneath it. By now, the damage had been done. He was little more than a disfigured shell, whimpering like a wounded rodent.

I stood over him and pressed the tip of my sword to his sternum. Sulfuric vapor bubbled upward from the searing section of his chest. "I know you can still hear me even with your ear burnt off. This will be the last time we meet. If you ever come near me or anyone I love again, I will not be merciful enough to send you to Hell. I've been alive for a long time, Winters. I know places to hide you where you will spend eternity suffering and no one will ever find you. You'll beg for something as sweet as Hell. Goodbye, you godless son of a bitch."

I plunged the sword into his chest. He slumped over, dead on the spot. I stood over his corpse, reached for my phone, and called Ling.

"It's done. Come get him."

Gabriel's penthouse downtown held all the familiar sights of the upper crust New Yorker—a doorman, an elevator with mirrored walls, a golden chandelier in the foyer, and the entire tenth floor rented out to him and him alone. He owned thousands of properties worldwide, many of them even fancier than this, but he once told me he had a soft spot in his heart for northeastern architecture.

He was sitting the den with freshly washed hair, a white towel around his shoulders, a burgundy robe, and a three-finger scotch in his left hand. By now, his wounds had been healed, but I could still see the echo of exhaustion on his face. He'd used a lot of energy repairing the damage the bomb had done. Internal bleeding was no joke, not even to the angels.

"Michael," my brother said, rising from his couch. He actually gave me a hug this time with a brief pat on the back. "How did it go?"

I shrugged, then took a substantial sip of his scotch. It burned smooth and smoky all the way down into my belly. "He broke my nose. I set him on fire with holy oil."

Gabriel snorted. "A good time was had by all."

"Tons." I sighed, nodding towards the hallway. "Where's Jordan?"

"In the guest room to your left. She went to bed about half an hour ago."

He paused. "She wanted to wait up for you, but I told her not to."

"Thank you," I said, handing him the scotch. "She's got enough on her plate without worrying over me."

"Indeed." He pointed to the bulky paper bag in my right hand. "A late night snack?"

I smirked, heading for the kitchen. "Something like that."

Gabriel's guest room — the first one, anyway — was hilariously oversized and lavish, just like everything else in his place. The bed sat up on a cherrywood four-poster bed frame with transparent curtains fluttering down from the top. Jordan lay facing the door, dead to the world, her raven hair already hopelessly tumbling out of its ponytail.

I brushed the gossamer curtain aside to have a proper look at her. No frown on her face for once. She slept peacefully. I bent and kissed her forehead before turning to leave.

"You're being creepy again."

I froze, and then bit back laughter. "Sorry. I've been working on it."

I turned to see her eyelids halfway open, as if she'd been just on the cusp of true slumber. "Did you get him?"

"And then some."

"Good man. Does that mean I can go back to my place tomorrow?"

"Yeah."

She yawned, snuggling the side of her face against the fluffy pillow. "Not in a hurry, though. This bed is awesome. You should try it."

I arched an eyebrow. She was half-sleep, so I should have let that slide, but I didn't want to. "Why, Miss Amador, are you inviting me into your bed? How forward."

"You were the one who gave me a goodnight kiss."

My cheeks flushed. She was the only person on this whole damn planet who could do that to me, and I hated it. "Fair enough. Now go back to sleep."

"Happily." I had reached the door by the time she spoke one last time. "And don't think I forgot about your promise."

I grinned. "Your Chinese food is in the fridge, madam."

"Marry me."

I chuckled before shutting the door.

"Maybe someday."

LUST

One of the cushions on Jordan's couch had a loose spring that kept jabbing me in the ass. The entire two hours I'd been here had been uncomfortable as a result. I really needed to convince her to get it fixed or replaced.

Heels clicked across the kitchen floor. I spotted Jordan out of the corner of my eye, one hand on her hip, the other buried in her shoulder-length hair.

"Hey, sorry, but can I bother you for a second?"

I glanced at her. She turned around, giving me a view of her nearly-naked spine, visible because of the half-zipped dress she wore. "I can't get this stupid zipper up all the way. You mind?"

"No, it's fine." I stood and walked over to her. She held her hair out of the way and I started carefully maneuvering the zipper back down towards her waist. The dress was black, short, and form fitting. Telltale signs that someone else had bought it for her, either Lauren or an old boyfriend. Jordan liked her dresses tight in the chest and loose around her legs. She had strange insecurities about her thighs.

"I can't believe Lauren's making me go on a blind date," Jordan grumbled for what had to be the thousandth time.

I shook my head. "Then don't go."

"I have to," she whined. "I have this…pathological need to please her."

I snorted. "How come you don't have that with me?"

"Because you're not a person. Ow!"

I pinched her side and felt an immense sense of satisfaction when she squirmed. "Could you be more ungrateful?"

"Fine, fine, I'm sorry. But it's different with you. You don't expect me to live up to your standards. Mostly because you don't have any for me."

She paused. "Actually, I kind of like that. Makes things less uncomfortable."

"Mm-hmm," I said under my breath, trying to keep my eyes from sliding down her shoulders to the gap the back of the dress provided. The straps were thin and crisscrossed over her chest, but she was a classy girl and almost always wore a bra. This one appeared to be strapless. Not that it was important.

Whoever bought her this dress had known about the network of scars along the small of her back, starting just where her hips met her side. They were courtesy of her Aunt Carmen, who I had to remind myself on a weekly basis not to hunt down and bury in a hole somewhere. The back of the dress only dipped down to the middle of her shoulder blades, hiding the rest. One thing that I always found myself wanting to ask was why she wouldn't heal the scars, but we were still in the early parts of our friendship. I could only pry so much.

"Well, you never know," I said. "Maybe you'll like the guy."

"Oh, won't *that* be great? Then I can lie to him too."

I hesitated, sensing a deeper problem. "Is that what's got you so stressed?"

"Sort of," she admitted in a softer voice. "It's easier if I keep my friend circle small. I feel less like a jerk that way."

"You're a lot of things, Jordan, but never a jerk." I finally untangled the zipper and slid it all the way up. She let her hair fall around her shoulders and smoothed her hands down her hips, turning to face me.

"Thanks. Here's hoping I don't disappoint."

I smiled, brushing a lock of hair behind her ear. "You won't. He'd have to be an idiot not to like you. Especially in this dress."

She sighed, pressing her forehead against my sternum—a newly formed habit of hers because of our height difference. I leaned against the counter behind me to make it a little easier on her.

"Are you sure I can't stay home?"

"You'll be fine. Plus, it's a free meal and if he's an ass-hat, we can eat ice cream and call him names when you get home tonight."

Jordan chuckled. "You're so mature."

She laid her hands on my waist, which seemed to be her version of a hug when she didn't feel like giving me a real one. I wrapped my arms around her, resting my chin on the crown of her head. We stood there for a while, saying nothing. The longer we stayed there, the more things I started to notice; like the faintly sweet scent of shampoo and conditioner in her hair, the satiny texture of the dress, and the way her body folded into mine like a missing puzzle piece, except not hard cardboard but rather soft curves instead.

My mind began to wander into less angelic places before I could stop it. My arms held her a bit tighter and my knee involuntarily shifted to between her legs. I had trouble focusing on something other than the heat of her. Before I knew it, my lips touched her forehead and she shifted in my arms, meeting my eyes. Was I leaning down towards her face or was that just my imagination?

"I'd better get going," she said, snapping me out of my thoughts. Immediately, I let go and slid my leg back, hoping she wouldn't notice what had just transpired.

"Yeah, have fun."

She disappeared into the bedroom to grab her purse and jacket before leaving the apartment. I rubbed my face with both hands and then ran my fingers through my hair. No big deal. Gabriel had told me there would be tests.

I definitely needed to start studying.

LUST II

Buying Jordan an ice cream cone was the worst decision I ever made.

There was nothing on television that particular warm night, so she suggested heading to the park to get some air. We decided to walk there to avoid paying cab fare and the musty unpleasantness of the bus, and along the way she spotted an ice cream parlor. As per usual, we argued like preteens about who paid for them, but I managed to win for once. My poison was always Rocky Road. I could eat it every night if it wouldn't be considered gluttonous. Jordan went for vanilla with a fudge swirl.

As we headed for the park, I ate my ice cream quite happily and finished it in less than five minutes. Jordan didn't. She spent about six to eight minutes on hers. I knew this because it was the longest six to eight minutes of my life.

I hadn't spent a lot of time around the opposite sex, not even when I thought I was human. Women liked me well enough, but even back then I stayed away from relationships because of my memory loss and general confusion about where I was going in life. I didn't exactly know a lot about little things they did that affected me in unprecedented ways.

For instance, some people bite their ice cream. Jordan was not one of those people. She was methodical about how she ate it. She licked the slowly melting sides first to make sure it wouldn't drip down onto her fingers before diving into the actual ice cream. She sucked the top of the scoop to soften it a bit.

My stomach did a double somersault. I stared at my shoes with determination, but I could still see everything in my peripheral. She alternated between slow licks and small nibbles. Her tongue always went from bottom to top. Her full lips would get smeared with white and then that damned tongue darted out to clean them. Then she made a delicious purring sound and the process started all over again.

At some point, she noticed my hunched shoulders and burning red face. "You okay? Brain freeze?"

"Yeah," I said weakly. "Ate it too fast."

She shook her head. "You should learn to pace yourself. It's not a race."

The blood in my cheeks felt like liquid fire. She had a disturbing habit of saying things my mind turned into double entendres.

We approached the stoplight across from the park. Jordan only had maybe a mouthful of ice cream left, to my relief. However, the soft treat had sunk down into the waffle cone shell and she needed to extract it. She held it up and stuck her tongue inside, swirling it around the edges until it came free.

I walked right into the crosswalk pole.

She gave a start as I backed up and rubbed my sore forehead. "That was graceful. What's the matter with you?"

"Nothing," I growled. "Just eat the damn ice cream so we can go."

She frowned, still suspicious of my behavior, and crunched on the cone until it was all gone. Then she licked her fingers clean and showed me her dainty digits.

"There. Happy now?"

"Ecstatic," I deadpanned. "Let's go."

The crosswalk light changed and we walked across the street towards the park entrance. We were about halfway there when I noticed her shoulders were shaking and her lips were rolled inward as if she were hiding a smile.

"What?"

She finally faced me and I was close enough to hear her stifling laughter. "I, uh, I take it you've never seen a girl eat ice cream before, huh?"

I was wrong before. Liquid fire was inaccurate. More like lava. I avoided her gaze and walked briskly so she couldn't see my mortified expression. "I have no idea what you're talking about."

She jogged behind me, trying to keep up, mirth evident in her voice. "Aw, come on, don't be like that. I'm just kidding!"

"Shut. Up. Jordan."

"It's totally fine if you thought it was hot. That's a normal biological reaction for a guy. Do you need me to give you the birds and the bees talk? When a man and a woman love each other very much—"

I whirled on her. She stopped, surprised at the abruptness of the movement. I caught her right arm and lifted it between us, my face still completely serious.

"You missed a spot."

"What?"

I then lifted her hand to my mouth and slowly licked a leftover glob of sweet vanilla ice cream off of her palm. Her jaw dropped. I smiled, lowered her arm, and then walked away.

LUST III

"Pick up. Pick up. Dammit, Gabriel, pick up the phone or so help me God I'll put your Jaguar into a trash compactor—"

"Hello? Michael? What on earth is the matter?"

"I need to see you. Now."

"Gracious, brother, what's happened? Are you hurt?"

"No," I said, raking a hand through my hair. "Just…look, I need your help. Can you meet me at the apartment?"

"Sure, I just got out of the shower. I'll be there soon."

"Thanks."

I hung up and continued my pacing in front of the couch. It would be foolish to actually stay here and wait for him to show up. However, there was no way in hell I was going back in my bedroom. Not after what just happened.

My hair was still damp from the ice-cold shower and I was shivering, so I threw on my robe and got a towel to dry it while I waited. Gabriel wouldn't be here for a while. I needed a distraction until then. I flopped down on the couch and turned on the television, not caring what would show up.

Naturally, the television revived on an especially graphic sex scene from *True Blood*.

I buried my face in my hands out of pure frustration. "Really? Now? *Right* now?"

I changed the channel to something I knew would be safe—Cartoon Network. Except it was about two o'clock in the morning, meaning Adult Swim was on. About thirty seconds of a *Robot Chicken* skit didn't make me feel any better. I switched to Boomerang instead and managed to calm myself with the carefree innocence of some early 2000's era cartoons.

Finally, a knock came at my apartment door and I opened it. Gabriel had most likely had a late night, but he was still dressed to the nines in a slick black suit, salmon tie, and white dress shirt. If I hadn't been so distressed, I'd have made fun of him. Who the hell dresses like this in the middle of the night to go see their brother? Only Gabriel.

His golden brow was furrowed as he shut the door behind him. "So what is it? What's wrong? You've never called me in face-to-face this late before. Is it Jordan? Is she hurt?"

"No, no, it's not like that," I said as I resumed my pacing. "She's fine."

He let out a rushed sigh and then sat on my black leather loveseat. "Thank the Father. Please sit down, Michael. You're making me nervous."

I sat on the couch and clasped my hands together. "Alright, what I'm about to tell you is probably the most uncomfortable thing I've ever had to tell another person. I apologize in advance."

Gabriel continued looking befuddled, but he nodded all the same. "What is it?"

I raked a hand through my hair, avoiding his gaze. "I…may have…accidentally…had a sex dream…about Jordan."

Silence. Thirty seconds' worth of it. Gabriel lifted a hand to his face, covering his mouth, and I swear to God, he choked on a laugh as he said, "Pardon me?"

My face lit up with a blush like the Festival of Lights in December. "You heard me."

"I couldn't have," the archangel said, his shoulders bobbing up and down with suppressed laughter. "Are you saying you called me from my home at two o'clock in the morning because you had a sex dream about Jordan?"

I glared. "How is that funny to you?"

He held out his hands in supplication. "No, brother, the fact that you had the dream is not humorous. The fact that you are taking it this seriously is."

"Why shouldn't I? I haven't been human in an incredibly long time, Gabriel. I shouldn't be having those kinds of thoughts about her. She's my friend. She's the person I'm supposed to be protecting, not some tawdry toy for my imagination. I've clearly been compromised by my human instincts and I need help to rehabilitate myself or I don't know what I'll do—"

"Michael. Listen to me. This is normal."

I eyed him. "Normal?"

He smiled and all the teasing had gone out of his voice. "Normal. Here, let me ask you something. How many other women have you spent time with in the last decade?"

I thought about it. Aside from some of my sister angels, none. "Just her, I guess."

"Exactly. You see each other almost every day. You have a meaningful relationship with her. She's important to you. Sex dreams don't always have to do with the act itself. The two of you are intimate with each other on a spiritual level. Sometimes the brain misinterprets these things unconsciously. It doesn't mean you are going to lose control and ravish her. It just means you are adjusting."

I scrubbed my face with both hands, growing agitated. "Okay, fine, then how the hell do I face her tomorrow? I mean…it was…pretty damn vivid, Gabe."

He cleared his throat. "I see. Well, that you will have to figure out on your own. But if it comforts you, she has probably had the same problem."

I looked at him then. "I'm sorry, what?"

Gabriel arched an eyebrow. "How have you been alive this long yet you know so little about the fairer sex?"

"I...honestly have no answer to that."

He chuckled. "I figured as much. Give yourself some credit, Michael. You've been doing well getting used to human life so far. You still have a long way to go, but you're not breaking some sort of cosmic law by dreaming about her. You have the good sense not to act on these carnal desires, right?"

"Right."

"Then you will be fine. The first six months are always the hardest part. Afterwards, you will look back on this and laugh. I promise."

I sighed. I still felt humiliated, but I did genuinely trust my brother's wisdom. After all, he'd been here since the beginning. If anyone knew the truth, it was him. "Thanks. Sorry I dragged you out here."

He patted my knee. "That's what brothers do. I wish you a...better night."

He waved and left the apartment. I locked the door, flipped off the television, and shuffled back to my bedroom.

I tossed the damp towel in the hamper and shucked off my shirt. My hair was still wet, but I'd deal with it. I had to go to work tomorrow. I needed sleep.

I turned to the bed and tried my absolute hardest not to conjure up mental images from the dream. No big deal. It was like Gabriel said. She and I were friends. She was important to me. It had nothing to do with romantic feelings at all.

The rumpled sheets greeted me with open arms as I collapsed face first on the mattress. I yanked the comforter up over my head and told myself to just sleep. Half an hour rolled past. Still not asleep.

Then, miraculously, my mind started to drift towards the edges of slumber. A woman's throaty voice calling me in the night. Delicate hands running down my spine. Long legs around my waist. Smooth dark skin. Lips pressed against my ear. Creaking mattress.

I sat up and tossed the covers off my head.

Sleep is overrated.

All hail insomnia.

GLUTTONY

"I'm going to die."

I chuckled and then stopped when it made my stomach clench. "Drama queen."

Jordan leaned her head back on the couch, rubbing her usually-flat-but-currently round belly with both hands. "We shouldn't have done this. Why did we do this?"

"You're the one who said we had to eat the entire batch before it went bad," I said, shooting her a look. "That's the only way we could justify making a new one."

She frowned. "You're supposed to be the moral one. Why didn't you stop me?"

"Because they're really good cookies."

"I know, aren't they?"

I let out another lazy laugh that made my pumpkin-chocolate-chip-cookie-filled gut hurt once more. "We've got to learn restraint at some point."

She waved one hand at the plate on the coffee table. "There's only two left. Should we go for it?"

"I thought you said you were gonna die."

"Yeah, but it's a good way to go."

I shook my head. "Fine. One each?"

"Why not?" She groaned and leaned forward as slowly as possible, reaching for the plate. With some effort, she picked up the cookies and handed me one, slumping back on the couch in relief.

"Cheers," she mumbled, taking a bite. I did the same. We lay there, chewing in silence. It was by far the most indulgent moment of my life.

Jordan finished hers first and let out a huge sigh. "I vow to never do that again."

"I vow to never let you talk me into doing that again."

"Sounds like a good deal to me." She fumbled around for the remote control and turned the TV on. I ate the final piece of my cookie and wiped my mouth with a crumpled napkin nearby. I closed my eyes and lay my head back on the couch, letting the random noise of the television consume the remainder of my attention.

After a minute or two, I felt the couch move and then the weight of Jordan's slender body across my lap. I opened one eye to look at her. She lay sideways with her head on the armrest, her long legs trailing down the other end, ankles crossed.

"You're gonna make my legs fall asleep."

She snorted. "Please. Like you're gonna get up any time soon."

I closed my eye. "Point taken. But you could've asked me to move."

I felt her shrug. "Didn't want to make the extra effort."

It took a lot of self-control not to smile. I didn't have to be a genius to know what she wanted. We had been in this strange bodyguard living situation for almost two months now and I'd picked up on nearly all of her non-verbal cues. Thus, she didn't say anything when I rested my hand on her stomach and started to rub it in small circles. After all, there was nothing in the rules that said I couldn't.

Or maybe I was just a glutton for punishment.

GLUTTONY II

As a warrior for God, there were a lot of things I had been prepared for over the centuries.

Babysitting was *not* one of them.

Especially when it was spontaneous.

"Hey, where are you going?" I asked as Jordan turned left out of the restaurant instead of to the right. "The bus stop is that way."

"I've gotta go pick up Lily."

"Lily?"

"Lauren's daughter. Lauren had to switch shifts and her babysitter's got a cold. I need to walk her home from school so let's go."

She kept walking. I caught up with her and didn't hide my indignation. "Wait, I didn't sign up for this."

"Yeah, you did," she said in a frank tone. "You're the one who parlayed with God to be my bodyguard. Suck it up, Commander. You can handle one afternoon with a six-year-old."

I stuffed my hands in the pockets of my leather jacket. "Yeah, it can't be all that different from hanging out with you. Ow!"

She whacked me in the stomach with the back of her hand. "She's a sweetheart. You'll be fine. What? Do you not like kids?"

"I like kids just fine," I grumbled as we came to a stop at a light. "I just don't like being in charge of them. They're tiny and so…breakable."

She arched an eyebrow. "And you have such big strong hands?"

I glared at her. She grinned. "Sorry, too easy. Don't sweat it. It's only for a couple extra hours, and then you can go sulk in your Man Cave in peace."

"I'm an archangel, not Edward Cullen. I don't sulk."

"Whatever you say."

It didn't take long to get to the elementary school. The long yellow buses were crowded up against the curb with their doors wide open to the squealing little ones. Jordan and I waited as waves and waves of them left for home, until eventually a little Korean girl in purple appeared. She had a Minnie Mouse shirt and black fluttering skirt, leggings, and buckled shoes. Her cheeks were round and she had one crooked tooth up front, but she was ten different kinds of adorable. Her face lit up as soon as she spotted her escort.

"Auntie Jordan!" Lily cried, flinging herself into the Seer's arms.

Jordan spun her and hugged her tight. "Hey, squirt! How are you?"

"Good! Where's Mom?"

"She got stuck working late, but she'll be home in a few hours." She adjusted the little girl in her arms and turned towards me.

"Lily, this is Michael."

I smiled. "Hey."

Lily's brown eyes widened. She tapped Jordan on the shoulder and then Jordan leaned in. The child whispered something in her ear and she laughed.

"No, he's not my boyfriend. He's just my friend."

Lily wrinkled her nose. "You can be friends? With *boys*?"

"Occasionally," she said, shooting me a sly look. I rolled my eyes. Figures they'd gang up on me.

Jordan put Lily down and then held her hand. "Alright, let's get going. What do you want your snack to be today?"

Lily shrugged. "Dunno. What do you think, auntie?"

"We had frozen yogurt last time and caramel apples before that. How about bubble tea?"

"Ooh, can I get a big one?"

"No, you bottomless pit. It won't be long before dinner."

I glanced at Jordan. "Bubble tea?"

"You've never had one?"

"Hence the question."

She waved my sarcasm aside. "It's like a milkshake. Sort of. You'll see when we get there."

We walked another block and a half to a Vietnamese noodle house. Lily insisted on giving the order to the guy at the counter herself, so she asked me to hold her up. She got a small strawberry-flavored one while Jordan got a melon-flavored to split with me. She had been right. It looked like a milkshake, but then I noticed there were little black dots along the bottom that looked like beans.

"Here," Jordan said after sticking a straw into hers. "Try it."

I hesitated. I happened to like Vietnamese food quite a lot, but I wasn't much for sweets.

"C'mon, it's really good!" Lily said, tugging at my jacket hem.

I lowered my mouth to the straw and tried it. Swallowed. "Weird."

I licked my lips. "But not bad."

Jordan smiled. "Odd. That's how I describe you to other people."

I sent her another withering stare and she giggled, leading Lily back out onto the street. Lauren had a one bedroom apartment in one of the more affordable districts of the city. From what I'd heard, she and her husband split about a year ago and had shared custody. Lauren kept Lily during the week and the father kept her on weekends. If it was hard on the girl, she didn't show it. She told us what she'd learned in school in between mouthfuls of the bubble tea and waved at strangers and tried to pet every dog that passed by her along the way.

We were about three blocks from Lauren's place when I noticed our tail.

At any given time, my attention was split between my human senses and the intuition I carried under the surface as an angel. Demons and various criminals tended to intersect in certain behaviors, particularly when following someone. Career criminals knew how to stay out of sight and keep their distance, as did the average demon. I recognized the same man across the street at the elementary school and at the corner after we left the Vietnamese place. He was good, but I knew what to look for.

"Hey, there's a comic book shop down the street from here. Ever been there, Lily?" I asked.

Her face lit up. "No. Can we go, Auntie Jordan? Please?"

The Seer glanced at me, confused, until she saw the expression on my face. I kept it neutral so Lily wouldn't think something was wrong. Jordan gave me a small nod and then smiled at the little girl. "Sure, why not? Oh, your shoe buckle is loose, honey."

As Lily bent down, Jordan angled her face towards mine. To anyone else, it would look like she was giving me a peck on the cheek. "What is it?"

"Someone's been following us," I said as quietly as I could. "Take her inside the shop and stay there. If anything looks suspicious, head for your place."

"Got it. Be careful."

Jordan squeezed Lily's hand. "Michael's going to run a quick errand, so it's just you and me for now, squirt."

Lily pouted. "Okay. Bye, Uncle Mike!"

I smiled warmly at her. We'd known each other less than an hour and she already considered me part of the family. Gotta love children. The sorry bastard tailing us was going to regret the very thought of endangering such a sweet kid. "See you in a bit, munchkin."

Jordan and Lily turned and headed down the street, away from the potential threat. The tension in my shoulders relaxed somewhat after I saw them go inside. Time to work.

I crossed the street once the light changed and observed the stalker in my peripheral vision. Black guy, six foot, white polo shirt, black slacks, shades, leather jacket, Chucks. Appeared to be late thirties. Toothpick clutched between his teeth. He stopped at the corner where I'd just been. This was the pivotal moment that would determine if he was after me or Jordan. I couldn't sense any demonic energy coming off of him, but a lot of demons knew to mask their signatures when they were after an angel.

A cold pit opened up in my stomach as he headed towards the comic shop. *Shit.*

I doubled back the way I came and kept twenty feet between us. I was too far away to see if he was carrying, but I bet money he was. Direct confrontation might force him to make a scene or take hostages. I needed to neutralize him before he got near the girls.

I cleared my throat and spoke in a low tone as I began to catch up with him. "Yea, though I walk through the valley of the shadow of death, I will fear no evil; for thou art with me. Thy rod and thy staff, they comfort me."

The first couple of verses made the man stop in his tracks. Aha. Demon. I suspected as much. His superhuman hearing became his Achilles' heel for that exact reason. Scripture was the equivalent of nails on a chalkboard to demons—it wouldn't kill them, but it sure as hell hurt, enough to give me an opening while he was distracted.

I walked faster, increasing the speed of the recitation. He started to twitch and glanced about trying to spot me. "Thou preparest a table in the presence of mine enemies; thou anointest my head with oil. My cup runneth over. Surely goodness and mercy shall follow me all the days of my life, and I will dwell in the house of the Lord forever. Amen."

Too late, he spun around. I grabbed the inside of his right arm as if we were shaking hands and simultaneously dug the edge of my knife into his ribs. He froze. I adopted a jovial grin for the sake of the people still walking on either side of us.

"Cyrus!" I said. "How you been, man?"

The demon coughed, smiling weakly. "Good, good. Nice to see you."

"We should definitely catch up. Can I buy you a cup of coffee?"

He swallowed and nodded. "Sounds good."

I linked our arms together and led him through an alley to our right, two stores down from the comic shop. As soon as we were out of sight, I dropped the act.

"Ten seconds, demon," I growled, shoving him against the brick wall behind him. "Talk."

He held up his hands. "I'm not here to hurt anyone. I swear."

"Nine seconds."

He licked his dry lips. "Word on the street is that you were the one who had the Spear of Longinus. You know how much it's worth. I'm a collector. Name's Virgil. I'm interested in the Spear, not your girl or the kid."

"She's not my girl," I said automatically. "But you were damned stupid to follow me while I was with her."

Virgil snorted. "When are you *not* with her?"

I jabbed the knife into his chest and he cringed.

"How long?" I demanded.

"How long what?"

"How long have you been after me?"

"Just a couple days."

I narrowed my eyes at him. "Do you even know who I am?"

"I just know what I heard, man. That's why I was tailing you. I've been trying to find out if you were the real deal."

"So what were you going to do? Convince me — an archangel of the Lord — to give a low level fencer one of the most powerful weapons in existence for money?"

Beads of sweat popped up along his forehead. "Not my first choice."

I stared at him. "You dumb son of a bitch. You were going to ransom Jordan and Lily off for the Spear."

"I wasn't—"

I lifted the blade to his Adam's apple. "Alright, alright! It's nothing personal. You angels forget that it's not like heaven down here. Demons like me have to fight to get street cred. If I could succeed where Belial failed, I'd be set for eternity and then some. Can't blame a guy for trying."

A nasty smile spread across my lips. "Oh, I can and I will. Do you know what happened to the last guy who threatened me and someone I was protecting? His name was Jean Winters. He's dead now."

"I get it," Virgil said. "You're the big bad angel to end all big bad angels. Now are you gonna kill me or let me go?"

I weighed my options. Broad daylight. Not the best idea to leave a body with so many witnesses about. Definitely didn't mean I'd let this moron off the hook, though.

"Hand or foot?" I asked.

He frowned at me. "What?"

"You demons only understand pain and misery. I'm not going to kill you, but I am going to teach you a lesson. So answer the question: hand or foot?"

Virgil sweated bullets for a minute or so. "F-Foot."

"Thank you."

I returned my knife to its sheath and slid it back in my pocket. Then I whipped out the silenced pistol hidden in the lining of Virgil's leather jacket and shot him in the left foot.

He screamed and crumpled to the ground, rocking back and forth clutching his leg. I opened the chamber and dumped the bullets down a nearby storm drain, then chucked the weapon several feet away.

"Consider that a warning," I said over the sound of his cursing. "The Spear is not for sale. It's out of your reach. Do yourself a favor and learn from this mistake. The next angel you meet might not be as kind."

I turned my back on him and started down the alley.

Virgil shouted after me, his voice shaking with both anger and pain. "You can't protect her forever, asshole! One of us is going to get to her eventually."

I stopped. My hands balled into fists. *Go back*, the soldier in me whispered. *Remind him of who you are. Show him your true nature. Maybe then he won't be so quick to insult you.*

I turned to see Virgil propped against the wall with one arm, glaring daggers at me. His demonic energy boiled around him like steam. "Seers don't last long. Not when there's so much we can do with them now. You won't be around every second of every day. You're just a man."

"You think I don't know that," I said quietly. "You think I'm so naïve that I believe I can always be there to stop scum like you? Of course not. Do you really want to know why I'm doing this, you sorry sack of crotch droppings? Because I'm immortal. I have all the time in the world. She doesn't. It doesn't matter if she's going to die someday. As long as I'm around, she will live her life the way she could have if she hadn't been born a Seer. I don't care how many of you come for her. I'll kill you all if I have to."

Virgil laughed. "You're dense if you think you can stop us."

I bared my teeth in a grin. "Try me."

He said nothing as I walked away and disappeared around the corner. Maybe I was dense. Wouldn't be the first time someone accused me of such.

Lily and Jordan were in the DC Comics section, sitting on the small couch and leafing through a Batgirl comic. All of the fury inside me drained out as I saw the pair. I stood at the edge of the aisle and rested a forearm on the bookshelf, not wanting to interrupt just yet. Jordan was smiling and explaining Cassandra Cain's backstory to the child, who listened with rapt attention.

A long time ago, I would have found the idea of watching over a Seer to be an insult to my abilities. Human life was fleeting. They came and went like flowers in a meadow. Now that I was in the trenches, so to speak, I understood why Gabriel preferred to spend his time on Earth alongside them. Moments like this one were why we fought the demons, why we bled for mankind, why we were tasked with protecting them.

A tendril of black hair spilled forward and Jordan tucked it back behind her ear. Then she glanced up and saw me. I nodded to indicate the problem had been resolved. A fond smile touched her lips and she patted Lily on the head, whispering something in the girl's ear. Lily leapt out of Jordan's lap and ran for me, grabbing my hand to tug me over to them. She insisted that I sit and she would read the comic out loud, as long as I promised to provide the voices of the male characters. I didn't mind.

The most startling thing was what went through my head in that instant.

I could get used to this.

GLUTTONY III

"Michael."

"Hmm?"

"It's four in the morning."

"And?"

"And you've been watching *Breaking Bad* for like ten hours straight."

I blinked my suddenly rather dry eyes and tore my gaze away from the television. "But Jordan...*it's so good.*"

She pressed one hand over her face. "I know it's good, but you're eventually going to have to sleep. And eat. And function someway similar to a human being."

"But...Walter White, Jordan. *Walter White.*"

Jordan finally walked past the couch and hit Pause on the DVD player. "It'll be there tomorrow, I promise. Now go to bed."

"Just one more episode—"

"NO."

ENVY

"Hey."

I turned in my chair to find a black guy around my age — well, my human age — standing next to my table, looking a bit apprehensive.

"Michael, right?"

"Yeah."

He relaxed into a smile and offered his hand. "Kyle. Jordan told me to meet you guys here. Where is she?"

I shook it. "She's running late. Should be about five minutes or so. Take a load off."

He took off his leather jacket and draped it over the back of the chair before sitting down. Soft jazz oozed over the room. I let the live music sink in and told myself to keep my cool.

"So you're Jordan's best friend, right?"

I shrugged. "Sort of. Lauren's her other best friend. I'm new at this gig."

Kyle grinned. "Ah. Well, since I've got you here, you mind if I ask you a couple questions about her? See, I like her, but I'm not sure how she feels. She's sort of distant, y'know?"

I shook my head. "You have no idea. I'd be glad to help. Hit me."

"She doesn't strike me as a flowers kind of girl."

"No, she's not. You'd be better off bringing her food. She eats like a football team. She doesn't like candy, but she does like chocolate. Try to get the Swiss kind, if you can."

Kyle nodded. "Got it. And what about movies? Any in particular she likes?"

"Mostly horror. Especially if it's bad, because she likes to make fun of stuff, sort of like riffing them."

"Great. Does she have any subjects she's touchy about?"

"Family."

"Family, really? What about it?"

"Let's just say she's got a rough past. I'd avoid asking her about her folks unless you guys really hit it off."

"Okay. Anything else?"

I paused, thinking. "She doesn't drink. We've been working on her alcohol dependence so be careful about taking her to a bar. She likes to dance, but only at certain clubs. She sucks at pool, but she still likes to play it every once in a while. She loves live music and concerts, and she actually buys CDs instead of downloading everything like most people do. She doesn't like to go swimming because it makes her hair frizz. She loves kids, but doesn't seem to want to have any of her own anytime soon. The only technology she can operate properly is a computer, and even that's limited. She has to have coffee every morning or she'll turn into the Wicked Witch of the West. And no matter where she sleeps, she has to be on the left side."

I glanced up from my drink to see an expression of awe on Kyle's face, which immediately made me realize I'd gone on far longer than I should have.

"Wow," he said in a hushed tone. "You really do know a lot about her."

I offered him a sheepish smile. "You asked."

He eyed me. "Are you sure there isn't something I should know about you instead of her?"

I stared at him and started to answer, but then I felt a hand on my shoulder and turned to find Jordan standing next to me.

"Hey, boys. Sorry I'm late."

She walked around the table and sat next to Kyle, glancing between the two of us.

"So did you find something to talk about?"

He and I met eyes, answering simultaneously.

"Not really."

ENVY II

"And now I know how Brangelina was born."

Jordan nodded sagely. "It's an important right-of-passage as a human being."

She hit the 'Mute' button and slumped back against the end of the couch. A couple strands of dark hair sprouted from her loose ponytail. I caught sight of them in my peripheral vision. I always had the urge to push her hair back. Maybe it was a neat nick thing. Not sure.

We watched the credits to *Mr. & Mrs. Smith* slowly scroll up the screen. I lay my head back on the squishy cushion. Her legs were strewn over my lap while mine trailed onto the floor. Never enough room for both of us — it was a smallish couch, after all — so we often ended up sharing. It was also hot as a jalapeño's ass in here, so we were both in shorts and sleeveless shirts. The guy wouldn't come to fix her air conditioning until tomorrow. We should have relocated to my place, but laziness was a driving factor in our friendship. That was how we ended up watching the movie instead of going out.

Not long after Jordan began theorizing a way to remove the DVD from the player without actually leaving her seat, a thought crept into my head and out of my mouth before I could stop it. "Three-hundred and twelve, though. I mean, wow. Even for Angelina Jolie, that's a lot."

Jordan shook her head. "It was how many people she'd killed, not her sex number."

"True. While we're on the subject..." I cut my eyes across at her. "What's *your* number, Jordan?"

She blinked once, slowly, and then adopted an indignant look. "Are you kidding me?"

I shrugged. "It's a legitimate query."

"No, it isn't."

"Why not?"

"How is that any of your business?"

"We're friends, aren't we?"

"So?"

"So does Lauren know?"

"Yes."

"Then why can't I?"

"Because Lauren's been my friend for over two years. You haven't hit two months yet. Sorry, but my life's not an open book."

I scowled. "Oh, come on. I'll tell you mine."

She snorted. "It doesn't count when your number is zero. Nice try, but no."

"It's got to be really high or really low for you to be this defensive."

She crossed her arms beneath her chest. "I'm not being defensive."

"Then just tell me."

"I can't."

"Because...?"

"We're supposed to be drunk when we do this, you know."

I stared. "Pardon?"

"That's how it goes," she said, stretching out a little further. I lifted my hands from where they'd been resting on her calves until she settled.

"After we've both had a little too much to drink, you start asking me questions I normally wouldn't answer. These things have a rhythm."

"What things?"

"Male-female platonic friendships."

"Uh-huh," I said. "So does the drunk version of you answer the question or does the drunk version of me have to guess?"

She wrinkled her nose. "Guessing usually goes horribly wrong. Too high, and it sounds like you think I'm a slut. Too low, and it sounds like you think I have no game."

I choked on a laugh. "Jordan Amador has game? Why was I never aware of this?"

She jabbed me in the thigh with her heel, glaring. "*Callate*. I've got loads of game, thank you very much."

"Objection. The prosecution would like to see some proof."

She paused, and then her eyelids lowered into a sultry stare. "Well, it is almost two in the morning and you're in my apartment in basically your underwear."

She had a point. Sort of. "I'm your bodyguard. Doesn't count."

Jordan groaned, tossing her head back. "I hate you."

I chuckled, letting the conversation lapse into a natural silence between us. The faint white glow of the still-rolling credits bathed us in pale light for a while. I drew absent patterns on her knobby knees, drifting off into the ether until something else materialized in my brain. Something equally private and invasive that I should have kept to myself, but to hell with it.

"Can I ask something personal?"

"No," she said without looking at me.

I angled my face towards her, my voice careful. "Was Terrell your first?"

She stilled. Her entire body just stopped anything resembling motion — breathing, the way she shifted her legs when my hands found a ticklish spot, the small movements of her fingers resting in the crook of her arms — everything. I expected her to get mad. After all, it really was none of my business, but I was curious. There were a lot of things I didn't know about modern women. Jordan was sort of my guinea pig.

"Why would you ask me that?" she whispered.

I shrugged. "Maybe I'm a masochist."

"I thought I made it clear I don't want to talk about this."

"You did. But I've noticed there are a lot of things bothering you that you don't want to talk about."

"Your point being?"

"Maybe if you talk about them, they'll stop bothering you."

"Who died and made you my therapist?"

I thought about it. "You did."

She sighed. "Point taken. If I tell you, can we drop the subject immediately afterward and eat ice cream?"

I bowed my head, though she didn't see it. "I swear, m'lady, it shall be done."

"Good. Yes, he was."

"How did he react when you told him?"

"I didn't," she whispered.

I sat up straight, my jaw hanging open. "What?"

Jordan squirmed, her arms tightening around herself. "I couldn't. It just…made me feel too vulnerable. I was eighteen, remember? We do a lot of dumb stuff at that age."

My eyes shut for a second. I knew enough about a girl's first time to know she shouldn't have done that. Guys could always tell. "Was he angry?"

"Furious," she said with a hollow laugh. "In retrospect, it was a selfish thing to do. I guess I didn't tell him because in our culture, virginity is such a huge deal when it pertains to a girl, but not as much to a guy. Society acts like it's some kind of sacrifice when a girl loses hers and the guy becomes her new god. I didn't want that to happen. I still wanted to be me after it was over."

The pain in her quiet tone was raw. It took me almost half a minute to notice I'd been stroking her leg in comfort. "Were you?"

"Yes and no."

"Did you regret it?"

"Yes and no."

"Do you think he did?"

"I promised myself I'd never ask that question."

"Sorry," I said.

"It's okay."

"No, I mean it. Sorry for prying. I didn't think the conversation would head in such a painful direction."

Slowly, her arms uncrossed themselves. Her fingers toyed with the hem of her tank top. She still wouldn't look at me, but I'd expected as much. What I didn't expect was her question.

"Does it bother you that you're not allowed to be with anyone?"

I studied her for a long moment, mulling the question over in my head. "Sometimes. On the one hand, I'd probably be a terrible boyfriend."

"Pfft, no argument there."

I pinched her calf and she flinched. "On the other hand, part of me wonders what it's like. Especially since the human race is so obsessed with not being single most of the time. Makes me wonder what all the fuss is about."

"Fuss," she said with a chuckle. "That's a nice way of putting it."

"Thanks," I said, rolling my eyes. "I'm sure it's for the best."

Silence floated down over the two of us. I couldn't tell if it was comfortable or not. It just happened.

"I don't think you'd be bad at it," she said after several minutes.

"Bad at what?"

"Boyfriending."

I grinned. "Is that a word?"

"Yes. I'm human. I know these things."

"Right. Thanks for the compliment. For what it's worth, you're probably not a bad girlfriend either. I get what Terrell saw in you."

Again, she snorted. "That was never the problem. It's what he didn't see in me."

Curiosity ate a hole in my stomach. "What didn't he see?"

She sighed. It was quiet, but I knew in that moment that my time was up. "I think I'd like some ice cream now."

"Yeah," I said softly. I squeezed her leg once, just for a second, and hoped she knew what that meant. She lifted up to let me pass and I retreated to the kitchen to fetch the aforementioned dessert. A lot of layers to the Jordan onion. Wonder if I'll ever peel them all. Or if I even should.

I brought Jordan a bowl. As I sat down, she scooped up a glob of the ice cream and ate it. Her tongue darted out and licked away some cream from her bottom lip. She sucked the spoon clean and made a small delighted sound.

I focused on my own bowl of frozen goodness and pretended it was the ice cream that had made my mind go blank for a second.

ENVY III

Public transportation was not my favorite thing in the world, but for Jordan, I tolerated it. I'd seen far more horrible things in my time. Though I admit crazy smelly hobos weren't high up on my list of things I wanted to experience as a newly minted human man.

I stood leaning against the bus stop sign with a folded-over paperback copy of *American Gods* in one hand, keeping Jordan in my peripheral. She sat on the bench, engrossed in the first volume of *Sin City*. I couldn't have reached her if I dumped a trash can over her head. Jordan took her reading very seriously. She didn't even flinch as a twenty-something whizzed by on his skateboard and sent her an appreciative look. Couldn't blame the guy. Her black skirt had ridden up a few inches so one could see just a peek of thigh. She wasn't awful curvy, but she did have nice gams.

"Ahem."

I glanced to my right to see a brunette girl standing there, bouncing a little on her heels to see over the edge of the book held up near my face. "Someone's got good taste in novels."

I grinned. "Lucked into it, actually. Was looking for something else and this caught my eye."

"Yeah, Gaiman's one hell of a storyteller," she said, tucking a ringlet of hair behind her ear. "And by the looks of things, you're getting to a really juicy part of the book. The ending's spectacular. It's worth the ride, trust me."

"Whoa, spoiler alert."

She grinned wider, exposing dual dimples in her cheeks. Her eyes were that rare kind of topaz blue. I guessed she was in her early twenties, based on her black leggings, purple tank top, and the tattoo of Legolas on the inside of her right forearm. Orlando Bloom as Legolas, that is.

"So, um, are you new to this area? Haven't seen you before. I usually catch the bus back from the gym every week."

"Yeah, I haven't been on this side of the city long. I'm only here because of her."

I jabbed a thumb at Jordan, who didn't even glance up. I doubted that she heard me, not with Marv gathering up her attention.

The girl's smile wilted around the edges. "Oh."

A thought popped into my head. A stupid one. Not that it was unusual for me. "It's not like that. She's like my sister. My extremely short-tempered, annoying, unappreciative sister."

"No, that just sounds like a regular sister."

I laughed. "Only child. Wouldn't know."

"You're lucky that way. I'm Abby, by the way."

"Michael."

The mechanical monster known as the city bus rumbled up to the side of the curb and burped out a cloud of mud-colored exhaust. The doors flung open and a few people hopped out.

Abby chewed her bottom lip. "Well, this is me. You coming?"

"No, that's not our route. Sorry."

"Don't sweat it. Maybe I'll see you around. Later."

"Bye."

She hurried onto the bus with her yoga mat tucked firmly underneath her arm. I watched the bus amble off into the streets and returned to my book. It was a full thirty seconds before Jordan said anything.

"…sister? What? You from Alabama or something?"

I rolled my eyes. Still, this was the second time she'd ever referenced the fact that we kissed. I wanted to poke further into the matter, but not in public. "What? It's not like you're my girlfriend."

"Didn't say I was. But still, even a girl like that could tell you're full of crap."

"A girl like what?"

"You are aware of the fact that she was trying to pick you up, right?"

I frowned. "She was just being friendly."

"Uh-huh."

"What? Men and women can talk to each other without there being underlying sexual tension. It's a thing. I think."

"How long have you lived on Earth again?"

She had a point. I didn't even believe myself. "It's a moot point either way. I didn't want to crush her hopes. Besides, you're not exactly my type."

"You have a type? Since when?"

"Since shut up."

Her lips parted into a victorious grin, yet her brown eyes never left the pages in front of her. It drove me absolutely insane when she won arguments, which was far too often.

"Maybe I like short girls who eat frozen yogurt and practice yoga as opposed to moody average-height girls who eat bacon every other day and yell at fictional British people on the BBC."

She glared at me then, offended. "Did you watch that *Sherlock* pilot? How could I *not*?"

"Not my point. Maybe I'm not allowed to date, but that doesn't mean I don't have a type."

"Well, you're not my type either, pretty boy, so I guess we'll just have to live with it."

I couldn't resist. "Is that why you let me get to first base?"

She whapped me in the side with the graphic novel while I laughed. People gave us funny looks. I didn't mind.

"Oh, come on. Admit it. You were at least a little bit jealous that she was hitting on me right in front of you."

Jordan groaned. "She had no idea we were even friends until you brought it up."

"What kind of *tsundere* are you? Aren't you supposed to get all offended when girls throw themselves at your ridiculously handsome platonic companion?"

"One more word and I'm pushing you in front of the next bus."

"Well, this is what you get when you make me watch *Ouran High School Host Club*."

"Shut up and read, *baka*."

BONUS CHAPTER: GLUTTONY

When my phone rang after midnight, it was almost never good news.

I awoke in a frantic daze, snorting in the most unladylike fashion as I tried to detect the foreign noise resounding through my bedroom. My hand slapped around the nightstand to silence the rousing techno chorus of Right Said Fred's "I'm Too Sexy," a ringtone that could only mean one person.

"What d'you want, Michael?"

"Heeeeeey, Jordan. You —*hic*—up?"

Wait, what?

I opened my eyes, sitting up in bed. "Uh, no. Why do you sound like that?"

"Like what?"

"You're slurring."

"Pssssssssssssh —am not."

There was a brief scrabbling sound, like someone tried to take the phone away. I heard another familiar male voice, this one considerably less slurred. Stan, one of his band mates. "Give me that, you dumbass. Jor? That you?"

"Yeah, what's up?"

"So, uh, he told you we went to a party downtown, right?"

"Right."

"He, uh, may have challenged Casey to do shots."

My eyebrow twitched. "Of what?"

"…water?"

"Stan."

"…tequila."

I palmed my forehead. "How many?"

"Lost count after ten."

"Excellent. Let me guess. You don't want him to try and get into his apartment this drunk."

"Yeeeah. Look, I'm sorry to bother you and all, but you know he's got work in the morning."

"I know. Tell me he has enough for cab fare."

"He can't find his wallet."

"Well, of course. Do you?"

Movement again, as if he were checking. "Yeah, I got it."

"Give the cab driver my address."

"I will. Thanks, Jor."

"Whatever." I hung up, slipping the warm comforter off my legs. So much for my comfy night alone.

About twenty minutes later, the doorbell rang. And rang. And rang. Thirty times.

I yanked the door open and immediately slapped Michael's hand away from it. "Would you knock it off?"

"Sorry," he said, breathing an enormous mouthful of alcohol fumes in my direction. "Wasn't sure you heard me the first time."

I grabbed him by the front of his t-shirt and dragged him inside, then kicked the door shut. "I heard you the first dozen times, you moron."

"Hey, I'm not a moron," Michael whined, scowling at me as I locked the door.

"Yes, you are. What happened to your wallet?"

He shrugged. "Dropped it somewhere. I'll find it in the morning."

"If you live to see morning," I growled, stomping past him to my couch. Navy suede pillows adorned the burgundy cushions. I tossed them aside until there was enough room for my stupid best friend's lanky ass and pointed.

"Sleep. Now. You have to be at work in the morning."

His scowl deepened, those green eyes narrowing. "You're not the boss of me, y'know."

"I am tonight, pretty boy. What the hell is the matter with you? Casey drinks like a fish. What made you think challenging her to taking shots was a good idea?"

He sniffed, an arrogant tone creeping into his voice. "I'm Commander of Heaven's Army. I can hold my liquor, I assure you."

"Uh-huh. By the way, you're missing a shoe, Commander."

He glanced down at his feet. Wiggled his toes. Noticed one of said feet only had a sock on it. "Ah. Well spotted, madam."

A smile threatened to sneak its way onto my lips. *No. Don't reward him.*

I marched over and hauled him behind me by the wrist. He could have easily stood his ground, but Michael still believed himself to be a gentleman, so he'd never fight back. He stumbled once or twice on the way, and I didn't figure out why until it was too late. Untied shoelaces plus couch plus the two of us equals a painfully awkward landing.

I hit the couch on my back and he didn't have the reaction time to catch himself on his hands. His huge frame squashed me underneath him and our foreheads smacked together. Crackling pain shot through my skull.

"Ow," I choked out, shoving my hands against his shoulders. "Michael, geez, get it together. You're crushing me."

He pushed up on his palms, frowning. "Sorry. You okay?"

"I'll live," I grumbled, rubbing my aching head. "Now do you understand why I quit drinking?"

He nodded, looking unnaturally sober all of the sudden. "I mean it. I'm sorry. I know this must be hard for you since it's only been close to two months since you quit."

I adopted a gentler expression. The guilt on his face immediately subdued my annoyance. He may have been tipsy, but I didn't have to go overboard scolding him. He was my friend, after all. "It's fine. Really."

"Good."

I expected him to scoot over, but he didn't. He sighed and dropped his head onto my shoulder, molding our bodies into one lumpy mass. I didn't dare move, too shocked by the sudden intimacy. Each tequila-tainted breath steamed over my ear, my neck, across my clavicle. He left his arms on either side of me, his long legs trailing between mine. He felt solid and hot everywhere, like a slice of the sun.

"The other angels ask me why I do this, you know."

I licked my dry lips, unsure of where this conversation was going. "Do what?"

"Protect you," he said softly. "Stay on earth. They think it's beneath me. A babysitting job. An insult to my military career."

He nuzzled my neck, burying his nose behind my ear and into my already-tangled black hair. My heart slammed against my ribs, excited, scared, confused, frantic. Michael wasn't the type to keep secrets, but he rarely spoke about his relationship with other angels save Gabriel. The tequila had loosened his tongue. I found myself wanting to know a little more about him, even at such a cost. Stupid. Selfish. Gluttonous.

"It probably is. It's child's play, but…" He trailed off, either drifting towards imminent sleep — bad for me because

I couldn't lift him on my own — or waiting for me to fill in the blank.

I debated with myself, chewing my bottom lip. "But what?"

He inhaled, which swelled his long upper torso for a second or two. It felt…interesting. "I miss heaven. I miss the air. I miss the light. I miss the sounds, the voices, the peace. Human life is unremarkable. It's ridiculous. Paying taxes, working retail for terrible compensation, dealing with the petty attitudes of others…it's enough to drive a man to drink."

He exhaled another scorching blast of air across my bare skin. "But I'm not lonely here."

My eyes widened, and I was happy he didn't see it. Michael was always so confident and upbeat. It never would have occurred to me that he had insecurities. He was just so…*Michael*. Debonair, dashing, never flummoxed or flustered.

He shifted his body upward. In his drunken state, he didn't quite notice what that one movement did. He wore a pair of ratty blue jeans with the knees worn out and a heavy black belt. Michael was about five inches taller than me, and a hell of a lot bulkier. Muscles flowed across him from his neck to his broad chest to his surprisingly narrow waist and toned legs. We'd fallen on the couch missionary style, embarrassingly enough, so it left our hips out of alignment. When he pushed onto his forearms, it dragged his waist all the way up, past my thighs, my bellybutton, my abs. It had been years since I'd felt that delectable heavy presence above me.

I couldn't help it. My flesh was weak. A muted groan of pleasure slipped out of my parted lips and he was too damn close not to have heard it. He lifted his head slowly until he stared down into my face, his brows drawn in a flat line, green eyes fixing me with a stare I couldn't classify in my distracted little pea brain. My arms lay on either side of the couch, limp and useless like wet noodles. *Damn it.*

"I guess I have you to thank for that," he said in a husky voice.

I swallowed. Hard. It hurt all the way down into my belly. "You're welcome."

Michael's hands drifted down to either side of my waist, accidentally brushing my legs — unhidden by the boxer shorts I wore to bed. I knew the rules. He knew the rules. Angels were forbidden from engaging in anything romantic with human beings. No kissing. No sex. No bases in between.

Yet there he was, leaning his face towards mine, his seawater eyes catching the faint moonlight from the window, rooting me to the spot. Fresh adrenaline pumped through my veins. I broke out in cold sweat all over — a ridiculous notion, considering how feverishly warm his body had made mine. *Do something, Jordan. Anything. Open your mouth and say something.*

My lips parted, but no sound came out. He'd sucked the air right out of my lungs with those quiet words and that heady look that I was stupid enough to think was for me. *Remember the alcohol. Remember the rules. Remember that he isn't yours. Remember.*

His breath curled against my upper lip, down one side of my cheek. My eyes fluttered shut. *Memory is overrated.*

"Good night, Jordan," he whispered, inches away from kissing me.

He sat all the way up in one fluid motion on the other side of the couch. I didn't move a muscle. It took at least eight seconds for me to register that he'd curled up and fallen asleep.

I closed my eyes, pressing my palms into them until red swirls danced before my vision.

Stupid.

Selfish.

Gluttonous.

Moron.

Acknowledgments

To my mother, whose endless enthusiasm for my work has inspired me in my darkest hours. I've thrown so many pity fiestas for myself and you always stuck with me through them. I couldn't have done this without you, and I don't ever intend to, no matter what happens in the future.

To my father, whose patience rivals that of a monk. You haven't given up on me yet. You're the Alfred to my Batman.

To my brother, who always made a point to remind me that I am in fact talented despite being a neurotic weirdo with a thing for forty-something actors. I'm glad to share my nerddom with you.

To Sharon, who has a thousand plates spinning at once and yet somehow still found the time to read my silly novels and offer insightful, beautiful, and helpful things to say about them. Your feedback is beyond invaluable.

To my family—Aunt Z.B., Mikey, Krystal, Uncle Mike, Uncle Mark, Aunt Nette, Darryl, Meagan, Layla, Uncle Jim and Aunt Vivian (God rest your souls), Tye, J.D., Gabrielle, and Tatiana, and so many others who know who they are to me—you're the best. I couldn't have become the woman I am without your love, support, and many, many hilarious holiday adventures.

To my friends, who have stood by me despite all the evidence pointing to fact that I am a total loon: your support means more than I can ever say in any language. Thank you for hanging in there. You didn't have to, and I know I'm a prickly pear, but you saw something in me that was worth sticking around for, and I appreciate it.

To my few but faithful fans, thank you. Just…thank you. You gave me a chance. I hope to someday make you proud.

To Christine Savoie, my book cover was driving me up the wall before you so kindly came along and made this gorgeous piece of art. Thank you. You are the shining example of benevolence, and I hope to work with you again in the future.

To Katie Litchfield, the wings you designed for Michael on the cover were beyond perfect. They're practically flawless. Thank you so much for letting me use them.

To Jennifer Troemner, you continue to make me the happiest lady ever by editing my work. You know these characters almost as well as I do and I'm so glad that you continue to offer me the best advice on how to make my work shine. Thank you.

To any stranger who has trekked with me through this literary journey, you are awesome and stunningly attractive, I must say. Thanks for hanging in there. I truly hope you enjoyed what you read, and if you feel so inclined, please drop a review on its Amazon or GoodReads pages.

Author's Note

Love doesn't conquer all. Love chases after you with a club, bashes your skull in, and then drags you off into a cave.

Mind you, I've never been in love, but if dating is any indication, then my simile (or is it a metaphor? My God, *how long have I been out of college?*) is probably accurate. It's impossible to truly describe the process of falling in love—or in lighter cases, like—with someone, but I gave it a shot anyway with this little adventure. I don't know if it was a successful enterprise (ENGAGE!) but I certainly hope that readers were able to glean something from it other than the fact that Michael is a very violent man and you should probably never ever threaten him or anyone he cares about.

Writing *The Deadly Seven* has certainly been a challenge, as I've never been able to replicate true brevity except for fanfiction. As the cliché goes, you've got to know when to fold 'em and that is way harder when you're writing stories that aren't supposed to be long and involved like chapters. However, this author's note isn't just me tooting my own horn—I'm actually trying to say something here.

New authors, don't stay on the playground with the other kids eating paste. Go out into that big scary field and spin around like Maria singing the hills are alive. Find something ambitious and run it down like Liam Neeson in *Taken*. Strap your dreams to a chair and threaten to electrocute them if they don't comply. That is the only way you will be able to survive in the cut-throat business of writing and publishing. Most importantly, though, do what you love and ignore the crazy voice in your head that says no one cares. Someone always cares. If people can read dinosaur porn fanfiction (sadly, no, I am not shitting you), then they can read and love your work. It may not be today or tomorrow, but if you write something of quality and you love it, others will too.

To you glorious denizens of the reading world, I simply ask you keep doing what you're doing. Love books. Collect them. Hoard them. Build a giant castle with them in your front yard and call it Fort Kick Ass, at least until the writers of *Archer* try to sue you. Share them. Review them. Pass them out to strangers like handfuls of candy. You're doing God's work. Or Satan's. Or Cthulhu's. I don't judge.

My life may not have turned out the way I hoped it would, but I have found that I am never happier than when I'm buried beneath the warm, friendly pages of a book. Unless that book is *Changes*. *I'm coming for you, Jim Butcher.*

Point being, do what you love. Always.

-Kyoko M.

Read on for a special preview of

She Who Fights Monsters

Book Two of the Black Parade series by Kyoko M., available
for purchase July 22, 2014.

CHAPTER ONE

JORDAN

"I have to go to work."

"Mm-hmm."

"The bus leaves in fifteen minutes."

"Mm-hmm."

"...I can't leave if you don't stop kissing me," I said in a mildly amused voice from around the lips of my husband who had managed to trap me against the kitchen counter. He towered over me with his six-foot-one-inch frame, his long sinewy arms content to rest on either side of the counter by my waist so I couldn't wriggle away. It was a nuisance yet somehow pleasant. A conundrum, if you will.

I thought my words had finally got through to him when he pulled away for a moment, but his head dipped down and his lips found my neck, making my poor knees wobble. I could feel the roughness of the stubble that had grown on his chin since he hadn't shaved yet. His dark brown hair tickled over my collarbone, sending involuntary shudders down my spine. Normally, when he cooked breakfast he pulled his hair back into a short ponytail, but I suspected he'd taken it down with the intent of seducing me. Crafty bastard.

"I'm not stopping you," Michael drawled against my throat. His baritone voice made the hairs on my arms stand at attention. There was maybe a centimeter of space between our upper bodies. He bit down softly at the point between my neck and shoulder. I jumped, gripping the counter for strength.

"You're blocking my exit," I said.

He finally rose to full height, smirking at me with those plush lips, arrogance beaming down from his sea-green eyes. "And you're stalling."

He stared at me. I stared at him. I sighed and grabbed two handfuls of his shirt, jerking him down to my mouth.

"I'm gonna get fired."

Half an hour later, my best friend Lauren Yi was shaking her head when I scampered into the restaurant and clocked in as quickly as possible. Mercifully, Colton was nowhere to be found, but he'd still know I was forty minutes late since he was the owner. I'd be in for it later and I knew it. The restaurant had been hit with the usual lunch rush, so I had to get ready as soon as humanly possible.

"This is the third time in a week you've been late," she reminded me as I walked towards the lockers in the break room. I popped mine open and checked my reflection in the mirror, piling my mussed black hair into a loose bun.

"I know, sorry. The bus was late."

Lauren rolled her eyes. "Are you really pulling that one on me?"

I glanced at her, keeping my face blank and innocent. "What?"

"Your skirt's on backwards and you've got pancake mix on your sleeve." She arched an eyebrow and then crossed her arms.

"He caught you in the kitchen again, didn't he?"

A flush of heat rushed up my neck and over my cheeks, thankfully hidden by my brown skin. I tied my apron on and cleared my throat, keeping my voice level and guilt-free. "I have no idea what you're talking about."

The Korean girl lifted the apron and turned my skirt the right way, brushing off the remainder of said pancake mix. "It's a sad day when Jordan Amador has more of a life than I do."

"Should I be flattered or insulted by that?"

"Both. Now get out there and wait tables, you shameless harlot."

I batted my eyelashes at her. "Love you too."

She stuck her tongue out at me as we walked back onto the floor and started greeting customers and taking orders. It never ceased to amaze me how quickly I could switch into Waitress Mode. Without thinking, I became amiable, even a little charming on my better days—a direct contrast to my actual personality. Lauren had once dubbed me a "cranky, antisocial hermit crab" and it disturbed me how accurate that description had been at the time. Michael had done a remarkable job of reversing the worst aspects of my behavior over the past year.

After I took care of a couple of teenagers and a large group of people who had just gotten out of church, I greeted a redheaded man in a hunter green suit and black tie sitting by himself at a window booth. "Hi, what can I get you?"

His brown eyes scanned the menu, his voice a little shy. "What would you suggest?"

I lowered my pen and pad. "Well, what kind of things do you like?"

He shrugged. "No preference, really."

"I recommend the fish and grits. The fish is fried whiting and the grits are cheesy and thick, just like down South."

"South?"

"Alabama, Mississippi, Georgia, and the like. I've never been that far down, but my boss insists it's much better than up here," I continued with a playful roll of my eyes.

The redhead folded up his menu and handed it to me, smiling. "That sounds good. Thank you, Jordan."

I scribbled down his order and smiled back. "No problem."

I gave the slip to the kitchen and grabbed some cleaning supplies to clear off a table in my section. Lauren came to help, taking the salt, pepper, Tabasco sauce, and napkins off of the table before I wiped it down.

"Who's the redhead?" she asked.

"No idea. Never seen him before."

"He's not part of the usual Sunday crowd. He seems…very out-of-town-ish, especially with that suit. By the looks of things, it costs more than half of my closet."

I flashed her a grin. "Well, you do have a bad habit of buying knock-off Gucci."

She scowled. "Those who shop at thrift stores shall not throw stones."

"It's economical, dammit!"

She rolled her eyes at me, handing me the spray bottle of Clorox.

"You're married to the lead singer of a rock band. You should be able to afford decent clothing by now."

I pursed my lips, squirting the bleach on the table. "We have better uses for the money than clothing, thank you very much."

"Condoms?"

I whirled, aiming the spray bottle at her face. "I'll do it and say it was an accident."

She giggled, pushing my arm down. "Relax, Dirty Harry. Or would that be Clean Harry since you've got Clorox?"

"Ha-ha. A comedic genius you are not." I finished cleaning off the table and replaced the condiments and napkin container. One of our chefs called for me and I brought the food to the customers. I took the fish and grits to the redheaded gentleman, who was staring out the window as if distracted.

"Here you go. Enjoy!"

"Thank you."

The lunch rush came and went like the tide— seemingly overwhelming at first, but manageable to the trained eye. I didn't notice anything out of order until I returned to the seat that the redhead had been in to find I had a rather substantial tip waiting for me.

"He left you *a hundred dollars*?" Lauren screeched from behind me and grabbed my shoulder to look over it. I held the bill between my hands, my mouth hanging open and getting dustier by the minute.

"I...he...maybe he didn't have change?" I sputtered. I searched the sidewalk outside the restaurant to see if he was out there, but he had disappeared.

My best friend threw up her hands. "I don't get it. You come in late and yet you're the one standing there with a fresh hundred bucks. Do you have a leprechaun stuck to the bottom of your shoe or something?"

Sheepishly, I glanced underneath my foot. "...No?"

"Ugh, I'd hate you if I didn't love you so much." Lauren sighed, scooping up the empty plate the mysterious redhead left behind. I tucked the tip in the front of my apron, staring blankly out of the window. I started to hand her a glass, only to drop it as something caught my eye across the street.

A plump woman in her early forties stared back at me. Her hair was black and curly around her round face, and her brown eyes were full of worry. I knew her — not from Albany, but from the pages of a manila folder I had poured over rigorously for the past month. Erica Davalos.

A murdered Seer.

"Jordan, what's wrong?" Lauren asked.

I hid my distress, stepping over the bits of broken glass. "Nothing, sorry. Just a bit clumsy today. I'll go get the broom."

I hurried to the break room and grabbed a broom, but I didn't head back out. Instead, I snuck out the rear entrance that led into an alleyway and stuck my head around the corner, signaling for the ghost to come towards me.

"Hi," the ghost woman said when she was within earshot, her voice light and apprehensive. "My name is Erica."

"Yeah, I know."

She frowned, tilting her head. "Excuse me?"

"My name is Jordan Amador. I'm a Seer."

"A Seer?"

"Yes. It's someone who can see and hear ghosts, angels, and demons. Long story short, they're the descendants of the original twelve disciples. I've been trying to solve your murder for the past month-and-a-half."

Her eyes widened. "Oh my goodness, I had no idea. I've just been wandering around for the longest time looking for someone to help me."

I offered her a small smile. "Well, you've come to the right girl. I get off work in a few hours, so I want you to stay in this area and meet me out front at six o'clock, okay? We'll get everything sorted out, I promise."

"Yes. Thank you so much."

She turned on her heel and headed back towards the street as I went inside to clean up the mess I'd made. Lauren was still looking at me funny, but I convinced her it was a mere case of the butterfingers. After all, Lauren knew nothing of my other life, and I had to keep it that way for her own safety. Rules were rules. Even if I didn't like them one bit.

After I dumped the glass in a trashcan, I sent a text to my other best friend, Gabriel, explaining that he needed to meet me at my apartment after work if he was in town. The last time I spoke to him, about a week ago, he and Raphael were in Haiti doing volunteer work. I didn't know if they were still there, but I figured they would have to pull some strings to get to me in a reasonable amount of time. It helped that Gabriel had his own private jet.

I tried not to show my impatience for the remainder of my shift, but at the end of it I scurried out of the door and met Erica outside, reaching into my grey duster for a pen and my trusty little notepad. I also got out my Bluetooth, which I hardly ever used to for real. It was just my cover to avoid drawing attention to myself. Normal people wouldn't be able to see or hear her. I didn't want to come off as a crazy lady talking to thin air.

"Alright, give me everything you remember from the top and don't spare any details, even if you think they're minor," I told her as we walked towards the bus stop.

"I remember my last name, Davalos, and that I'm from Raleigh." she said.

"I can't believe you walked all the way here from North Carolina. You're definitely a trooper." I scribbled the information down along with a brief description of her facial features and clothes. She wore a lavender button-up shirt and grey slacks beneath a black sweater, no jewelry. Her feet were, of course, missing. All ghosts were like that because they were no longer tied to Earth but suspended between the living world and the spiritual world. The clothing was a result of her internal self-image.

"And I remember that I was a kindergarten teacher and I loved my kids. I have a daughter. She's seven."

"Okay. Is there anything you can tell me about your death? Anything at all?"

"Yes. I couldn't see his face, but I heard his voice. It was saying something in Latin. I studied it back in college so I actually remember what he said quite clearly."

I winced. "My Latin's a bit rusty, but Gabriel should be able to translate for us. Go ahead."

She took a deep breath and closed her eyes, her brow furrowing. "It went like this: *Qui recipit lumen superius, a fonte lucis non aliam doctrinam necessaria, etsi concessum est.*"

It took me a moment to get all the spelling correct—I could read and write in both English and Castilian Spanish, but Latin was tricky—and by the time I finished, the bus arrived. We climbed aboard and sat in the back to stay out of earshot of other riders. Usually, I'd wait until we were home to ask all these questions, but an entire month with no new leads made me overeager.

"He was repeating it like some sort of chant while he stood over me, lighting the place on fire as if he were...I don't know, trying to purify it," she said, frowning.

I wanted to reach out and touch her hand in comfort, but it wouldn't do her any good. It would pass right through her and send chills through me. Only poltergeists were solid, and they were rare. I had only met two of them in my entire life.

"Well, that says a couple things to me," I told her. "The killer is well-read, perhaps a linguist, if he was pronouncing all of that well enough that you remembered it. Two, we're looking for someone with a religious background. You're not the first dead Seer that I've been investigating."

"Really?"

"Sadly, yes. Over the past five months, there have been five others murdered in different parts of the world. Four of them were stabbed in the chest, laid on the floor, and then their homes were burned to the ground. One was strangled and his car was set on fire. It always happens on the eve of their Awakening, just like I'm assuming yours did."

"Awakening?"

"That's when your powers mature. It happens at a different time for every Seer. Mine didn't hit until I was eighteen. Yours came a bit late, it seems."

"How is it possible that he knew when it would happen for me?"

I shook my head. "We don't know. Gabriel is supposed to appear whenever someone's powers awaken, but this serial killer somehow knows exactly when and where these Seers surface and always beats him there. However, you are the first Seer soul to stay behind. The others passed over into Heaven and they gave the same report as you each time."

"So what's going to happen to me?"

"We're going to find out what your final wish is and that will set your soul free so you can cross over for your final judgment."

"We?"

I smiled. "My friends and I. They're archangels."

A mixed look of astonishment and skepticism crossed her face, making my smile widen.

"Really?"

"Yes, really. Don't worry — you're not the first person to say that. I have a, um, complicated sort of life. You'll meet them when we get home."

A few minutes later, we arrived at my bus stop and I led Erica to my humble abode. The apartment was nothing close to nice. It was smack dab in the middle of a crowded, shady neighborhood, squished between a liquor store and a barbershop. That was why it was so affordable.

We walked down the street and up a short flight of stairs to my apartment on the first floor, second room over. When I opened the door, there were two men at the kitchen table eating banana bread. The first was a blond man who was almost seven feet tall with sky-blue eyes dressed in an impeccable Armani suit. The second was a significantly shorter curly-haired Hispanic man with brown eyes dressed in a tan sweater vest over black slacks and a black button up shirt. I didn't panic. They had keys, after all.

"Jordan," Gabriel said as he unfolded his enormous frame from the chair after I shut the door.

"Hey, Gabe." He pulled me into a hug and kissed my forehead in the same spot as always — over my right eyebrow. "Good to see you."

I hugged Raphael. "Hey, Raph."

"Evening, Jordan."

I grinned as I noticed half of my homemade banana bread had vanished. "I see you've helped yourselves to my sweets."

Gabriel blushed. "I…did not eat lunch today. Forgive me."

The urge to laugh was immense, but I pushed it aside. "Just this once. I'm charging you for the next one."

I gestured to Erica, who seemed politely bewildered by the two men before her. "This is Erica Davalos. I met her outside of the restaurant a few hours ago."

The blond archangel bowed his head to her. "My name is Gabriel. I am God's Messenger here on Earth."

Raphael did the same. "Raphael. I am God's Healing Missionary. We are terribly sorry for the loss of your life, Mrs. Davalos."

"Why? It's not your fault some jerk-off killed me."

"I am responsible for facilitating instructions to new Seers. If I had arrived sooner, I could have prevented your death. For that, I am truly sorry." Gabriel's voice was low with shame. I could feel his sadness like a cold weight in my stomach and started to say something, but Erica did it for me.

"I don't blame you. No one's perfect, not even angels. I just want to make sure that my family is taken care of now that I'm…gone."

Raphael offered her an encouraging look. "Your husband and daughter are safe, Mrs. Davalos. They have found somewhere to stay and they are being watched over. Nothing will happen to them. I swear it on my honor as an angel."

"Thank you," she murmured, finally smiling again.

I withdrew the notepad from my pocket and flipped to the page with her name on it, then addressed Gabriel. "She remembered something that the other victims didn't when I spoke to her earlier this afternoon. You told me that they heard the killer chanting something, right?"

Gabriel nodded. "Yes, but we were never able to get a transcription."

"Now we've got one. It's Latin. Can you translate it?"

He took the notepad from me, his lips just barely moving as he read. "I know these words. It's an excerpt from *Paradise Regained*."

"What does it translate to?"

He took a second or two, as if trying to remember his English. "He who receives light from above, from the fountain of light; no other doctrine needs, though granted true."

"You've got a damn good memory, Gabe."

"Well, I did help dictate most of it for Milton in my earlier years. Still, this is a strange thing to chant while murdering someone."

"Why is that?"

"It suggests that this killer thinks that he is following orders from on high, perhaps that he has a superior knowledge or truth. The fountain of light implies Christ or God the Father rather than heaven itself. In my opinion, it sounds like he thinks that this 'truth' he has discovered is his only mission and that he will follow it without question."

"Great. There's nothing worse than a man on a mission. And it still brings us back to the same question…" I sat in the chair by the kitchen table, suppressing a long sigh. "Why hasn't he come for me yet?"

Erica spoke up then. "I don't understand. If you all work for God, can't He just tell you who is doing this?"

Raphael shook his head. "God will not interfere on Earth until the Rapture. He charges the angels with solving any problems between heaven and the world below it. He believes that it will bring us closer together if we work as one without His help."

"Oh." She paused. "That sucks."

I grinned in spite of myself. "I know. I said the same thing when I found out."

"Regardless," Raphael continued, though he was smirking. "I will escort Erica back to her home and help her find her final wish."

"Thanks. Be careful." He nodded to Gabriel and me before gesturing to the door. Erica waved to me before walking through the closed door while Raphael left the traditional way.

I ran my fingers through my hair. My skull felt fit to burst.

Gabriel sat down across from my chair, watching me. "What's going on in that head of yours, Jordan?"

"I don't get it, Gabriel. I'm not an exceptionally powerful Seer. Why is it that I've been spared and six other people lost their lives?"

"It's possible that whoever is doing this knows that your soul is bound to Michael's and that it would be nearly impossible to kill you without risking his own life. The other Seers led normal lives. You're living with a dyed-in-the-wool warrior."

I frowned harder. "But that's not right. I shouldn't get a pass just because I happen to be married to an archangel."

A soft chuckle escaped him. "Jordan, are you telling me that you're feeling guilty because someone has *not* tried to kill you? It's a far cry from your usual behavior."

I snorted. "Point taken. No one's tried to kill me in over a year. I'm starting to miss the adrenaline."

"Perhaps I could make an attempt on your life, if that would make you happy."

I had to smile. "Thanks, that's sweet of you, but I've got a reminder right here to tide me over for a while."

I touched the spot over my heart where an ugly brown scar lay beneath my button-up shirt where the Spear of Longinus had once pierced. I couldn't believe it had been over a year since my life changed forever. "Dying once is enough, trust me."

"Indeed." He went silent and a thought occurred to me.

"Tell me something. Why would this killer recite that passage in Latin? Wasn't *Paradise Regained* originally written in English?"

His brow wrinkled. "Yes, you're right. That is curious. Perhaps he knows that Latin was one of the languages most used by the angels in earlier times?"

"But what does that imply? Clearly, he knows about Seers and angels, or else he wouldn't be able to always disappear before you arrive. What's the connection?"

"Maybe he sees himself as the angel of death for these Seers? But, again, that leads to another question: why is he killing them in the first place?"

I massaged my left temple. "I'm starting to think I should start wearing an expressionless mask and a blue fedora."

"Pardon?"

"Nothing." I glanced at the clock on the microwave and groaned.

"Shoot, Michael's concert starts in half an hour. I'd better get dressed. You coming?"

"Unfortunately, I can't. I have other obligations for the night. Please give him my support."

"No worries. You're overdressed anyway."

He grinned as he stood. "I thought you had finally come to terms with my preferred attire after I bought you that Dolce and Gabbana dress for Christmas."

"It was lovely, but it's so nice that I'm afraid to wear it," I admitted. It was an evening gown the color of dark chocolate that was made of pure silk. Gabriel often invited me to his high class social events, but half the time I couldn't go because I could never afford the right clothes. He decided from then on to upgrade my wardrobe whenever he got the chance. It was beyond thoughtful of him.

He chuckled again before bending to kiss me on the forehead. "Good night, Jordan. I'll see you soon, hopefully with good news about the case."

"Night, Gabe."

To be continued in *She Who Fights Monsters*, available on Amazon July 22, 2014!

Cover image courtesy of Illustrated Romance.

Cover designed by Christine Savoie. Wings designed by Katie Litchfield.